Mary Slessor
Missionary Mother
Terri B. Kelly

journeyforth®

Greenville, South Carolina

Library of Congress Cataloging-in-Publication Data
Kelly, Terri B., date.
  Mary Slessor : missionary mother / Terri B. Kelly.
    pages cm
    Summary: "Mary Slessor was a missionary woman from Scotland
who relied on God's will and power to overcome hardship and danger
to be a missionary in Africa for thirty-nine years"— Provided by
publisher.
    ISBN 978-1-60682-630-0 (perfect bound pbk. : alk. paper) —
ISBN 978-1-60682-631-7 (ebook) 1. Slessor, Mary Mitchell,
1848-1915—Juvenile literature. 2. Missionaries—Nigeria—Calabar
Region—Biography—Juvenile literature. 3. Missionaries—Scotland—Biography—Juvenile literature. I. Title.
    BV3625.N6S5985 2013
    266'.52092—dc23
    [B]
                                                2013028972

Cover and interior illustrations by Craig Orback
Design by Craig Oesterling
Page layout by Michael Boone

© 2014 by BJU Press
Greenville, South Carolina 29614

JourneyForth Books is a division of BJU Press
Printed in the United States of America

ISBN 978-1-60682-630-0
eISBN 978-1-60682-631-7

15 14 13 12 11 10 9 8 7 6 5 4 3 2 1

To my husband, Allan, for sacrificing your time.

*Thanks to all my writing friends and mentors,
especially Yvonne Lehman and Cindy Sproles.*

Contents

1

The Move

Aberdeen, Scotland • 1857

The sun cast a faint light across the cloudy sky as nine-year-old Mary Slessor ran from McGrady's Pawn Shop,down the cobbled street of Aberdeen toward home. A chorus of tenor and bass voices singing off key echoed into the street as she passed the tavern. Was Da' in there? A dark amber glint seeped through the window, and the deep, raspy voices caused a shiver to run up her spine.

Mary turned and looked over her shoulder to get a glimpse of her father. She could only hope he wasn't. The clink of glasses and laughter from the crowded tavern made her stomach tighten like the fists at her sides.

A few minutes later, Mary hopped over the two steps that led into their small cottage and set the tied handkerchief of money in her mother's hand. The cottage was a large room with a fireplace, kitchen to the left and a small bedroom to the right. On one side of the kitchen a set of stairs led to a loft where the children slept.

"My Mary's as fast as fire." Mrs. Slessor patted Mary's red hair and poured the money into the jar. "This should help pay bills. Take Susan for a while."

Mary held two-year-old Susan's hand and joined her brother Robert outside. "Sit here, Sis, and we'll play school." Mary smiled at Robert. "I'm the teacher. You're the preacher."

Seven-year-old Robert jumped from the stump he'd been standing on and yanked Mary's long hair.

"Stop that!" Mary swatted at Robert's arm. "Do it again and I'll box the freckles off them fingers."

"Ah, Carrots, don't get so fired up." Robert stepped back up on the stump he used as a pulpit. "Hey, Sis, listen to my sermon for Africa. I'm going to be a missionary someday." He held his arms in the air and lowered his voice to sound like a preacher. "Repent, be saved, and come to the ever-loving arms of Jesus."

Mary looked up at Robert. "My turn to stand on the stump. I want to preach like you, because I'm going to be a missionary too."

"Girls can't be missionaries."

"Can too."

Robert smiled. "Tell you what. You can be my assistant. We'll work for Jesus' kingdom together."

"An assistant?" Mary thought about that as she handed her doll to Susan, who was crying. "Hold the doll while I help mother." Mary picked Susan up and carried her inside.

Mrs. Slessor stood at the pine table, chopping an onion. "Not much to go in the soup tonight. Will you start a fire, dearie?"

"Yes, Mother." Mary sat Susan on the floor near her mother and joined Robert to carry wood.

It was long past summertime, and Mary rubbed her hands to warm them. As she did, she accidentally scraped her knuckle across the bark. A drop of blood seeped from the cut. She rubbed blood from the scrape onto her dress.

A few hours later, dusk turned to darkness over the Scottish streets. Mary held Susan's hand as they climbed the steps to the loft. Susan snuggled next to Robert while Mary tucked a threadbare blanket around their arms.

Robert sniffed. "I'm still hungry. Can I have more stew? Mother scooped out the last of mine into father's bowl."

Mary put her hands on her hips, "Robert, when you're nine like I am you'll understand. There's never enough food. We must save supper for Da'."

"But . . ."

"We'll fill your belly in the morning. Listen. I hear singing. It's Da'." Mary held a finger over Robert's quivering lips. "Hush now and sleep." Mary hurried down the loft steps, over to the fireplace, and picked up her knitting.

"Who moved the steps?" Mr. Slessor yelled in a slurred voice.

Mrs. Slessor closed her eyes, looked to the ceiling, and mouthed a prayer.

"I missed the steps," Mr. Slessor called as he clunked over to the kitchen chair.

Mrs. Slessor hurried to help her husband. "Here's your supper, my dear."

Mr. Slessor slung his arm, knocking the bowl into the fire. "Slop's not fit to eat." He straightened, and the bones in his neck crackled like the fire. He yanked out his pocket linings. "I haven't a pence to buy a soda loaf."

The empty bottle in Mr. Slessor's pocket slipped onto the floor and shattered. Mary stared at her Da' to see if the spill would provoke him again. For a moment, she didn't dare breathe.

"Go get my soup!" he yelled.

Mary's heart felt like it would thump out of her chest. She wished her father would stop drinking. She prayed like she'd seen her mother pray. *God, are You really out there? Please protect us.*

Mrs. Slessor wrapped her arms around her husband's shoulders and helped him to his feet. "This way to bed."

Mr. Slessor followed the gentle leading of his wife. Mary helped her mother settle her Da' into bed. A puff of dust settled onto the wood floor as he fell onto the corn-husk mattress.

Mr. Slessor sighed and closed his eyes. Almost immediately, deep snores assured them he would not wake soon.

Mary watched her mother rub the apron covering her round belly. "You'll have another little brother or sister in a few months," Mrs. Slessor said, "And everything's a mess. Our life is a mess. If your father hadn't started drinking—"

"Don't worry, Mother. We'll find a way. I'll sweep the glass," she whispered.

Mary carried the mound of glass outside in her apron and dropped it into the fire pit. Mary remembered her Da' from a few years ago—a tall, cheerful man, with red hair the same as hers. Now his skin looked leathery like the shoes he used to make.

Angry, she scooped up a pile of stones and hurled them at the ash tree. *Why doesn't Mother get angry? She's a saint.*

Tonight wasn't the first time her father's anger had chased her outside. She thought of her mother's worried face. *I'll do whatever I can to take care of Mother.*

Mary climbed the tree and looked down where she'd been playing with Susan. *Why should Robert be the only one to go off to exciting places*, she wondered? Mary blew warm breath on her icy fingers as a few flakes of snow floated through the air. She climbed down the tree, eased the door open, and snuck next to Susan.

After a few hours of sleep, the scent of biscuits woke Mary. Mrs. Slessor stood at the kitchen table, rubbing a crystal pitcher with her apron.

Mary wiped her sleepy eyes.

Mrs. Slessor continued polishing. "Mary, your father has decided we should move to Dundee for work. He left to arrange for a cart."

Mary twisted the sleeve of her dress and listened.

"Dundee's a bigger city. He'll be able to make shoes or work in the mill." Mrs. Slessor paused. "Your father got on his knees and *promised* not another drop of liquor would ever touch his lips."

Mary looked at her mother's glistening gray eyes and wiped her own. She wondered if her Da' really meant it. He'd promised before. "That's good news, Mother."

The butter melted as Mary dabbed the tops of the steamy biscuits, but her appetite had left her. Mary bit her lip. They wouldn't know anyone in Dundee. But she had to help her mother. Mary tilted her face toward her mom and smiled. "Mother, I want Da' to be the way he used to be. Even if it means moving."

Mrs. Slessor wiped her hands against her stomach. "We'll need money to move. I have more crystal ready for you to take to the pawnshop." Mrs. Slessor wrapped the dishes in a cloth.

As the sun spread a marmalade glaze across the sky, Mary's feet crunched against the dry brown leaves covering the street. Horse-drawn carriages rolled past. She approached the tavern and wondered if her father would keep his words or drink them.

McGrady stood outside the shop. "Back so soon, lassie?" The gap-toothed pawnbroker sucked back saliva through his teeth, words whistling through the spaces. The eyebrow above his left eye seemed to twitch as he spoke. He waved his arm for Mary to go inside.

Mary set the collection of silver, crystal, and china on the wooden table and unwrapped the muslin cloth covering them. McGrady leaned across the rough wooden counter and rubbed his chin. "Your mother's selling a lot lately," he said as he examined the crystal.

"Yes, sir," Mary said. "We're moving to Dundee."

Pawnbroker McGrady scratched his scraggly beard. "Everybody's moving to work in the mills."

Mary held her hand out as he dropped the farthings into her palm.

"There ya go. Now be off with ya before the gangs are out. You don't want to get robbed."

She hesitated. That didn't look like enough money to her. She pushed her hand forward and eyed McGrady.

He pursed his lips and stared at Mary.

Mary stared back.

"Don't expect to get rich here," he said, and then dropped another coin into her hand.

Mary curtsied.

Outside she dried her sweaty hands on her skirt, as if she could wipe the evil of the city away. Mary's shoes click-clacked on the cobbled streets. With every step, the coins jingled like hope in her heart. Would Dundee save Da' from drinking and save her poor family?

2

Dundee, Scotland

1859–1867

Mary looked out the upper story window of their two-room apartment on Queen Street. Smokestacks from the nearby factory tinged the air with soot. Raw sewage, litter, and rats covered the streets.

Her mother had a baby boy and named him John. Her father kept his promise not to drink for a month and then lost his job as a shoemaker. He went to work in the mill until they fired most of the men to replace their labor with the lower paid labor of women and children. Now Mary's mother worked as a weaver to keep the family from starving, while her father drank every night.

Mrs. Slessor set a tin of shortbreads on the table in front of Mary. "Happy eleventh birthday, my darling daughter." Mrs. Slessor adjusted baby John on her hip. "Mary, you are growing up."

Mr. Slessor positioned himself in a chair and drew in a long breath that whistled through the slight gap in his front teeth. "You're old enough to work in the mill, my Mary. And spunky enough for it too."

"Yeah, she can outrun every boy on the street," nine-year-old Robert said as he chewed on a twig of peppermint. "I wish I was going to work in that big old building."

Mary's stomach tightened at the thought of working in the mill. "Who will mind John and Susan?"

"They can mind themselves like the rest of the Queen Street roughnecks," Mr. Slessor said.

Mary studied Da's clear blue eyes. He'd not been drinking today, at least not yet.

"My Mary will be running circles round those machines." Mr. Slessor gestured as he spoke. "Ya see, you pretend it's the Loch Ness monster you're feedin', and ya fill that loom with cotton until the whistle blares."

Mary giggled. Oh, how she loved to hear her father's stories.

Mrs. Slessor patted Mary's hand. "Darling, you can attend school after working half a day."

"That's all I want to do . . . learn to read," Mary said.

Mr. Slessor laughed. "You'll be a *halfer*—half a day of work and half a day of school."

Mary bit off a tiny bite of a shortbread. The birthday biscuit felt hard. She coughed and cleared her throat, but the lump in her throat wouldn't go away.

That night, she crawled into the bed and prayed. *Dear God, I want to go to school, but I'm afraid of getting hurt on the machines. Will You help me learn how to do my job?*

At Baxter's Mill, Mary worked as a piecer. She ran under and around the machines, tying broken threads on the spinning frames. But when the noon whistle blew, she met her mother outside for a bag lunch and then spent the afternoon in a cramped, dark room the mill used as a classroom.

The cuts on her fingers from the tight threads didn't matter. The exhaustion from working in a ninety-degree room didn't matter. She was learning to read and write, and that's all that mattered. She wanted to read the Bible for herself so she could share God's love with others. Even after twelve hours of work and school, she stayed up late reading her Bible and missionary stories, especially stories about David Livingstone in Africa.

Two years later, her brother, Robert, began working at the mill. Mary advanced from her job as a piecer to working as a power-loom weaver. By the time she was fourteen, she had learned to run the loom so well that her boss had put her in charge of two. This helped the family since her mother now stayed home with Mary's new baby sister, Jane. Mary worked twelve-hour days and attended evening school.

As she grew older, Mary's love for God grew. She taught Sunday school classes at her church. When Mary turned eighteen, Mrs. Slessor took the family to church to hear a missionary from Calabar, Africa. Mary's desire to be a missionary continued to grow, and she asked her pastor if she could teach at the church's new mission. If she served the children in Quarry Pends—the roughest section of Dundee—maybe she could be a missionary too.

Reverend Baxter sat behind his wooden desk and shook his head. "Gangs dominate the area in Quarry Pends. You'll be in a dangerous part of town at night, Mary."

Mary held her head high and tightened her hand around her Bible. "I'm not scared."

"I'll say yes only if you promise to have an elder walk with you."

Mary loved teaching at Quarry Pends and planning Sunday picnics for the children. One night as she walked alone toward Quarry Pends, Mary remembered her promise to Reverend Baxter. She felt confident she didn't need an escort to walk with her so she continued toward the mission. She had learned to ignore the gangs' sneers and didn't care if they threw mud at her, as they did even when she had an escort.

Mary thought through the plans for the evening as she walked closer. She'd tell the children the story of the prodigal son, and they would sing and run races. As she approached the door, a teenage boy with a gang behind came around the corner, walking straight toward Mary.

Mary looked directly into the boy's eyes. "Hello."

"Stop right there, redhead. This is our area." The unlit cigarette in his mouth bobbed up and down as the leader spoke.

Please be with me, Jesus. "Come listen to the stories," Mary invited. She stood still, hoping the gang would move so she could scoot inside the door.

The leader pulled a rope from his pocket, flashing a yellow-toothed grin at her. "I've got a game for ya." A lead weight anchored on the end of a rope flashed as it spun around toward Mary's head.

Startled, her insides knotted. She knew if she ran, they'd chase her. Her heart pounded faster and faster.

She stared into the leader's dark eyes, trying not to show any fear. The rope swirled past her head. Once. Twice. Mary stood stiff, praying the entire time, her fists held tight to her sides. *Fear no evil.*

The weight, heavy enough to cut her, twirled closer and closer.

"Look at her. She's not flinching!"

Mary caught her breath but stood steady. She knew the weight would slam her temple next. Just . . . one . . . more . . . whirl.

The leader raised his arm and caught the rope in mid-swing. "She's no sissy."

Mary took a deep breath and relaxed her shoulders while the gang members gawked at her.

"I think she's game, boys. Let's see what she has to say." He motioned for the gang to follow Mary.

The room filled with children. The leader kept his word and made sure the gang followed Mary's directions. Before the evening ended, Mary had shared the story of Jesus' death and resurrection with the teenage gang.

That night at home, Mary prayed. "Thank You, God, for Your protection. And thank You for sending the gang to the mission to hear about You. Please work in their hearts. And, Father, I know nothing is impossible with You. Is it possible for me to go to the mission field?"

Someday—she hoped, she prayed—she'd be teaching children in Africa.

3

Changes

1870

Twenty-two-year-old Mary Slessor looked down at her dead brother, Robert, lying in the wooden box in the middle of their apartment; she lifted his hand and gently rubbed the back of his knuckle with her thumb. His skin felt cool to the touch and smooth, like the soft leather on her old shoes. Mary repositioned his hand, folding it neatly across the other and bent forward, kissing his auburn hair. Her tears beaded on his forehead.

Mrs. Slessor stood next to Mary.

"Where's Da'?" Mary whispered.

"He couldn't . . ." Her mother hesitated. "He's not coming."

Mary watched as her mother leaned over the box and tucked a twig of mint behind her Robert's ear. Mary remembered how Robert had always chewed a twig when chopping wood, carrying water, or sitting by the fire at night.

The pallbearers, thirteen-year-old John and three of Robert's friends, lifted the plain pine coffin and carried it through the streets to the church cemetery. Mary held the hands of her sisters, fifteen-year-old Susan and eight-year-old Janie. Mary followed the reverend and her mother as they trailed behind the pallbearers down the green slope, past granite memorials, polished marble, and small crosses marking the remains of others born and buried in Aberdeen. A bagpipe bellowed as the procession approached the cemetery.

They stopped in a corner of the cemetery reserved for the poor, forgotten, and . . . now her brother. The branches of a large black Alder shaded the spot where the pallbearers set the coffin. Mary sat on a bench with Janie, who sucked on peppermints, her leather boots swishing back and forth against the blades of the grass. At last the bagpipe's raspy exhalation faded.

"One last look," Mrs. Slessor cried. Her mother's sobs made Mary feel even sadder. The reverend gave Mrs. Slessor a moment and then guided her away from the casket.

Mary stepped forward to stare into the wooden box one final time. "This box ought to be filled with Bibles, sailing along with you to Africa," Mary whispered. "Remember? You promised, 'I'll take you to the pulpit, to His Kingdom, and to the ever-loving arms of Jesus,' you said. How're you gonna take me now?"

Reverend Baxter draped the black mort cloth over Robert's body, tucking in the edges of the cloth as if he were a toddler going to bed. Her brother's body sealed in darkness, the pallbearers closed the lid and lowered the casket into the grave. Next to the bench with her family, Mary stood on her tiptoes and watched until only a corner of the casket remained in view.

Mrs. Slessor scooped a handful of dirt and poured it over the casket. Mary kicked loose a dirt clod with her boots, a bit of dirt seeping through the holes in them. Bending down, she gathered the rock-hard clay and tossed it into the grave; she threw it hard enough to cause the clod to split and break like her heart.

"The parish will pay for the cloth and all the other funeral expenses, Mrs. Slessor," the reverend said. "My condolences to your family. Robert would have made a fine missionary."

"I had such high hopes for him to be a missionary, but tuberculosis killed him." Mrs. Slessor's voice cracked as she spoke. "Why Robert?" She slowly straightened and smiled. "At least I have one more son. John will be the family's missionary now. Thank you, Reverend. Wish God had given Robert . . ." She paused to wipe her eyes, her breath shuddering. "'Tis reassuring to have such a dignified funeral."

Five months later, Mary and her family stood next to Robert's wooden cross. A purple thistle twined around his cross. The fall wind still held the breath of summer, but Mary felt a chill standing now beside her father's coffin. His body, weakened by years of alcohol, had not been able to fight the pneumonia.

The years ticked by in Dundee. Mary continued her routine of working, read all the books she could, attended church meetings, and taught at Sunday school and the mission. Janie turned eleven and started working at the mill along with Mary, Susan, John, and Mrs. Slessor. Then John came down with tuberculosis.

The doctor suggested, "Move John to a warmer place, and he might survive."

Prompted by the doctor's warning, the family scraped together enough money for John's ticket to New Zealand. Sadly, a telegraph arrived announcing John's death only a week after he'd landed in New Zealand.

Mary dug a hole and slid another wooden cross next to her Da's. It had been five years since her father had died. Thoughts swirled in her mind. *Both my brothers have died.*

Will You send me to Africa, God? For years she'd been praying. Did God want her to go?

In 1874, Mary read in the *Missionary Record* of David Livingstone's death in Africa. Now that Livingstone's death had been confirmed, the mission board needed missionaries to replace him. The possibility that she could fulfill her lifelong wish kept her awake at night thinking, planning, and praying. She'd never confessed her desire to go to the mission field to her mother. She had to convince her mother.

"Be with me, Father," she prayed as she walked home from work. Her hand trembled as she turned the metal doorknob. She remembered David Livingstone's motto—move forward and pray.

"Mother?"

Mrs. Slessor laid her knitting needles on her lap.

"Mother, I want to apply to be a missionary. I'm stubborn and hard working. I'll go anywhere the mission board sends me. I just need your approval."

"Why Mary . . ."

"Since I was a wee girl, I've dreamed of going to Africa. Robert and John are both gone. I believe God's calling me." Mary fidgeted with her hands.

Mrs. Slessor's face beamed. "Dear, I'd never stand in the way of God's work."

"I shouldn't leave you, but Susan and Janie are here to help."

Mrs. Slessor shuffled through her Bible and handed a sheet of paper to Mary. "This must have been meant for you, not John. Here's the application."

Mary held the paper tight. She was twenty-six years old. The dream she held in her heart so long was now in her hand, almost. Just one more step. She wasn't the wife of a minister. She wasn't highly educated. Would the mission board approve a mill girl from Scotland?

Then came the paperwork. Seven months of waiting and warnings.

"Mission work is hard. Why would you want to be around wild animals in the mission field? You're afraid of dogs, Mary."

After she'd sent in her application, the day for her interview with the Foreign Missions Board arrived. The warnings hadn't scared her, but Mary shivered with nervousness as she took a seat in front of seven church elders. Would they reject her?

The mission board elders sat around a large wooden table. Mr. Logie cleared his throat. "Your application is approved, Miss Slessor."

Oh, thank You, Jesus. Mary wanted to bolt from her chair and hug every one of the elders. But she stayed seated and tried to keep her shaking knees still.

"We have a need in Calabar, Miss Slessor."

Mary felt her heart thump faster. "Calabar, Africa?" That was exactly where she'd wished to serve.

"Yes, Miss Slessor, and we understand if you decline. Calabar is dangerous mission field."

"No, I mean yes—yes, I want to go. No, I won't decline. Danger doesn't deter me. God has answered my prayers." Mary clasped her hands together and pressed them against her heart.

"We're sending you to Edinburgh for training, then you'll leave late summer." One of the elders handed Mary two books, an Efik dictionary and Bible. "You'll need to study the language before you arrive, then listen to the natives. The most important job you'll have during the first year is learning the native language."

Mary trained as a teacher in Edinburgh for four months. She received more warnings from new church acquaintances. "Why Africa? Don't you know Africa is the white man's grave? Diseases, animals, or the natives will kill you."

"It's a greater honor to go where my Master needs me the most," Mary said. "My heart's on fire for the Lord."

After teacher training, Mary traveled home to Dundee for three weeks of family time and then on July 30 she wiped away tears as she waved goodbye to her mother from the window seat of the train in which she would travel to Liverpool, England. She wondered, if Robert or John had lived, would either of them be sitting beside her now? As a young girl, she hadn't been sure if God cared. But time had proven that God did care. Fifteen months had passed since she'd first turned in the application, and now a lifetime's secret wish was blooming into reality.

On August 5 she stood on board the *Ethiopia*, waving goodbye to a few Dundee friends who'd traveled to Liverpool to see her off—off to the hardest mission field of all, Calabar, Africa.

4

Journey to Duke Town

August 1876

Mary looked over the ship's edge at the churning water. Except for the first couple of seasick days, she had spent the past thirty-five mornings on the deck talking with God. *Thank You for answering my prayer. Will You help me do Your work? I don't know what to expect.*

The morning of September 11, the deep dark ocean waters changed to a muddy hue. As land came into view, the Thomsons, who were returning missionaries, explained the sites to Mary. "We're entering the Cross River Channel now that will soon carry us into the Calabar River. We will be in Duke Town later today."

Back home, she'd memorized the names of each town in the Calabar area—Old Town, Creek Town, Eknetu, Okofiorong, and Duke Town. "I wish this ship were filled with as many missionaries as the casks of liquor I've seen. The sight of the river makes me feel excited and fearful."

Mrs. Thomson gave Mary's hand a gentle squeeze. "Ships also bring guns and swords to trade with the natives. Unfortunately, liquor is the most common currency used to trade for the natives' palm nuts."

After watching her father's drinking all her life, Mary knew what alcohol would do to a person.

Lime-green birds shot out from the forest, water lilies dotted the river's surface, and broad gray-green trees rose right out of the water as the ship edged closer to Duke Town. "Looks like the roots are growing above the ground. They're gorgeous trees."

"Ah, yes, the mangrove swamp. Beautiful, but infested with mosquitoes."

At the Duke Town port, natives paddled around old ships in a variety of canoes, loaded with fruits or cloth.

"England left the ships here for traders to store palm oil or other goods that natives trade," Mr. Thomson said. "They're permanent fixtures. Some traders live on the old vessels. Other ships moor here for months at a time."

From the *Ethiopia,* Mary could see the mission on the hillside above the Calabar River. Several palm-thatched

huts and wooden buildings sat among a variety of fruit trees. Canoes paddled around the ships to trade or pick up passengers. The mission's boat, manned by six native men dressed in red caps, white shirts, and dark loin cloths, waited for Mary while she climbed down the ship's ladder, and then the crew paddled her to the beach.

Mrs. Sutherland, a missionary for twenty-seven years, greeted her first. Mary followed her up the hill to the mission house. Orange and lemon trees scented the air. The outside of the mission house was surrounded by beautiful gardens. At the mission house, she met Miss Fuller, a Jamaican lady who helped around the house. Twelve missionaries and several African teachers also lived in the Duke Town Mission House. Mr. and Mrs. Anderson, who were in charge of the Duke Town mission house, were on furlough.

"The Calabar River is a busy port," Mary said.

"Oh, yes," Mrs. Sutherland replied. "The villages along the river in Duke Town trade palm oil with the merchant ships," she said.

"Trading must keep the natives productive. That's wonderful."

"Not as wonderful as you would assume," Mrs. Sutherland said. "Most natives prefer to trade for guns, swords, and liquor, rather than the native money called brass rods. The problem grows because the river villages trade the alcohol and weapons with the inland villages, but they don't allow the inland villages to trade at the river themselves. Villages along the river monopolize the trade with the merchants and guard the rivers with guns. The inland villages don't dare try to come to the river to trade, or there would be war."

"There's so much to learn," Mary said.

"Yes," Mrs. Sutherland said. "The alcohol causes problems. The natives believe all the white people are Christians. So the natives believe the guns and alcohol are good since they come from white men. Of course, most of the merchant ships are not sailed by Christians, and trading liquor and guns is a profitable business."

The first day, Mary helped with the cooking and cleaning at the mission and learned a few words of Efik, the language spoken in the villages surrounding Duke Town. Around the supper table, she learned more of the customs of the West African tribes. Mrs. Sutherland invited her to visit an Efik village the next day.

"Each village is full of hundreds of people. You'll see slaves, free women and men, and the chief, lower chiefs, and their wives and children. The African system of law here is called Ekpe or Egbo. Although the chief is in charge of his villages, he still answers to Ekpe law."

Then Mrs. Sutherland showed Mary the small room where she would sleep. "We have to keep the bedposts in tins of kerosene; otherwise an army of ants would march right into bed with you."

Mary sat on her bed, looking through the window, marveling. She closed her eyes, listening to the frogs and insects serenading outside, her mind full of all she'd learned the first day. Slivers of light illuminated a beautiful red hibiscus bush beneath her window. She sniffed the jasmine-scented air. *Ahhh, what a heavenly smell. This place is so beautiful, how could anyone say Africa is man-killing country?*

The next morning, Mrs. Sutherland prepared Mary for their walk. "As you travel in the forest or bush, always clap or sing. Animals attack when they're surprised. Leopards are nocturnal, so they're usually curled up in a tree, sleeping. And pray, pray, pray that you never surprise a snake."

"Snakes?" Mary had been worrying so much about leopards, she'd forgotten all about the possibility of snakes.

"Just be careful where you set your hand. A limb could turn out to be a python. Don't be scared. You'll learn the bush," Mrs. Sutherland said.

"I'll pray," Mary said. She was sure she was doing the work God wanted her to do, but her stomach tightened at the thought of seeing a python or some other wild creature.

Led by three native men who worked at the mission, Mrs. Sutherland and Mary hiked a couple of miles along a narrow wooded path, climbing over fallen trees and wading through creeks. Finally, the jungle cleared into a flat, grassy area.

"The slaves are already working in the fields," Mrs. Sutherland said. "Most Africans are slaves to other Africans. Slavery isn't new in Africa. Each village chief owns hundreds of slaves and his lower chiefs own slaves as well. Neighboring villages attack one another, claim their land, their women and children, and then turn their captives into slaves. The more people a chief owns, the more power he has. In Africa people are property, and power comes only through property."

The men and women dug in the fields, pulling up bunches of long roots that looked like long, skinny potatoes to Mary. Mrs. Sutherland stopped to speak to each slave. The smell of smoke greeted them before they reached the village.

"Slaves rise early to cook. All the people you see moving about freely are far from free. Slaves do all the work," Mrs. Sutherland said.

In the village, round palm-thatched huts crowded together. Goats nibbled at grass and chickens strutted around. Children sat in a circle playing a game. The moment they noticed Mary, the children scattered into the bushes.

5

The Villages

Mary squatted and looked at the pile of beans left in the dirt from the children.

"The children use the bean pods for games." Mrs. Sutherland chuckled and pointed to a tree where the children were hiding. "I suspect they've never seen a red-haired woman before."

They entered a clearing at the center of the village. A large drum made from a hollowed-out log sat near a hut. "The people gather here for dancing and war preparations." Mrs. Sutherland winced as if she were in pain. "And sometimes for a palaver. A palaver is a meeting, and unfortunately, the result is a flogging or killing."

Women passed them, carrying water jugs or baskets of fruits and vegetables on their heads.

"How do they balance those loads?"

"They learn to carry the baskets when they're young. The baskets are balanced on a cloth they twist into a bowl shape. It's amazing what large loads they can carry."

Two other women used long wooden poles pounding in a large clay pot.

"They're mashing the cassava, the same vegetable you saw the farmers digging up in the fields." Mrs. Sutherland pointed to the pot boiling on the fire. "They add it to soups or pound it into flour. Tonight everyone will be served the meal from this large pot. Men eat first and then the free women. Children and slaves always eat last."

They walked further into the noisy village. "Up ahead is the women's section. Each village has a yard for the chief's wives. Most of the men have twenty or thirty wives."

"Looks like all the huts have fences."

"Wives are free, but the law requires the wives to stay in their yard. There is strict punishment for those who disobey," Mrs. Sutherland said.

"That's not freedom." Mary's eyes scanned the small and crowded fenced area of the wives' yards. The fence was built of tree limbs and sticks. "I'm surprised they stay in the fences. They don't look very stable."

Mrs. Sutherland and Mary stepped through the gate of the women's yard. Some of the women braided one another's hair, some argued, while others napped. Mrs. Sutherland stopped to talk. Her voice remained soft and pleasant, but the wives spoke loudly, gesturing toward Mary.

Mary wished she could understand Efik. She recognized only a few words.

"They wonder if you are real or a spirit."

The women's chatter grew louder. Several rushed to Mary and patted her arm and hair.

"They don't believe you're real," Mrs. Sutherland said.

Suddenly, a man slashed a whip through the air at the noisy women.

The whip snapped against a couple of their backs. The women cowered in the corner of the yard trying to get away. Satisfied at the sudden quiet, the man stomped away.

Mary gasped. "The wives look like they're locked in a prison and their jailer has just punished them."

Mrs. Sutherland nodded. "That was the chief, trying to quiet down the women. Husbands have authority to whip their wives."

The chief's swift punishment reminded Mary of her father's rages. She wiped away the sweat running down her neck from the heat and from her anger. She put her hands on her hips, thankful she could speak a language the chief could not understand. *I have to help the women in these villages. How can I, Lord?*

As they spent time talking with the wives, Mrs. Sutherland interpreted for Mary. Then they left and continued walking through the village, inviting everyone— free people and slave—to the church service.

Mrs. Sutherland led Mary past a hut surrounded by a high stick fence. Two large young women sat on the ground, eating. "This is the fattening hut for girls chosen to be the chief's wives. For a year, no work or exercise is allowed. A fat bride represents wealth."

"But some of the women in the wives' hut weren't fat."

"True," Mrs. Sutherland said. "Once married, the husband doesn't care if his wife eats or not. Many suffer from hunger."

At the next hut, the air turned rancid. Flies buzzed over piles of animal waste. Inside, a threadbare cloth covered a bulge in the ground, with fresh fruit and vegetables outlining the mound. Mary clutched her stomach and tried not to breathe. She had never smelled anything so horrible. She wanted to pinch her nose, but didn't.

A gangly man sitting next to the mound spoke to Mrs. Sutherland. She opened her Bible and read in Efik to him.

"This is their son's grave," she explained to Mary. The family has given all their food for the boy's spirit. They will starve themselves in order to have enough food for the spirit. The father says, when the mourning period is over, he will have the witch doctor sniff out the evil spirit and then hunt down his son's killer."

"The witch doctor might die just sniffing at it," Mary said, making Mrs. Sutherland chuckle. Then she asked, "Do they know the cause of his death?"

Mrs. Sutherland closed her Bible. "No. The boy could have had an undiagnosed disease, or a spider or snake bite. The cause doesn't matter. They don't believe the young are supposed to die, so someone in this village or another village will be blamed."

Mrs. Sutherland sighed. "We do our best to teach God's power over life and death. Fewer than two hundred natives are Christians. Even for the Christians, changing the beliefs they were raised with is a battle."

Mary waved a fly away and followed Mrs. Sutherland to another hut. "But our Savior died for us. If they believed, their lives would change."

"Yes, their lives would change. We've had a few hundred baptisms, but there are thousands of people to reach. Thousands who grew up believing in superstitions and witchcraft, not a real God." Mrs. Sutherland nodded as she pointed to a dead chicken. "Sacrifices." Blood stained the wooden altar.

At another hut, a hunched and toothless woman sat in a dirty yard. Beside the woman, more bony and starving women lay almost lifeless. The toothless woman kept her eyes on Mary.

"Another group of women mourning a husband," Mrs. Sutherland said.

Overhead, vultures circled the village. Even though the hot sun heated the air like a fireplace, Mary shivered. She felt lost for words. So many people needed help.

Just a few days ago, she couldn't imagine an ugly thing in Africa and now she'd witnessed so much sickness, starvation, and superstition. How would she be able to teach the people not to believe in evil spirits? The work felt overwhelming. How could she serve people who fattened brides and starved widows if she couldn't even speak their language?

Over the next month, Mary toured more villages with the Edgerlys, a missionary couple from Duke Town. In Adiabo, the women boldly touched her face, arms, and hair. Mary was scared until she learned the women were showing friendliness. In Ikenetu she marveled at the gorgeous sunsets, and in Ikot Offiong she witnessed a village nearly ruined by an intertribal war. On her trips, whenever possible, she'd throw off her boots and climb a tree.

Mary bragged to the other missionaries. "I've climbed every suitable tree around here." The Duke Town missionaries warned Mary, "Mrs. Anderson runs a strict house. She might not like your outdoor adventures."

Soon the Andersons returned from their furlough. "Everyone calls us Daddy and Mammy," Mrs. Anderson said, when she met Mary.

For evening worship services, Mammy Anderson arranged a small round table, covered it with a cloth, lamp, and Bible. On Sunday, Mary estimated nearly a thousand people filled the wooden benches, while more stood. She thought the natives singing hymns in their Efik language blended like the most beautiful choir she had ever heard.

Before they went to bed that night, Mammy Anderson assigned Mary the job as the mission's bell ringer.

"You're in charge of waking everyone up," Mammy said.

Mary didn't have anything to rely on to help her wake up . . . except herself. She wanted nothing more than to please the Andersons with her work. After her evening routine of Bible reading, praying, and writing letters, she prayed for God's help, determined she would get up in time to ring the wake-up bell.

After drifting off to sleep, she suddenly woke and bolted up. The light from the full moon filled the room. Thinking it was morning, Mary scuffled into her skirt, stuffed her arms in a shirt, and tore outside. Several yards from the mission house, she grabbed the jute rope attached to the mission's bell and pulled.

Happy she hadn't overslept, Mary turned to the mission house searching for signs of anyone—especially Mammy Anderson.

The moon illuminated the mission house, casting shadows across the chairs on the veranda. All quiet, Mary ran back to the mission house, her heart racing.

No one in the mission stirred except Mammy, who stood in the center of the kitchen in her housecoat. "Mary," Mammy chuckled. "Your nightgown is hanging out from under your skirt and your shirt's on backwards."

Mary looked at her haphazard outfit.

"Dear, it's the middle of the night." Mammy Anderson led her toward the bedroom. "We'll have to get you an alarm clock to help."

6

King Eyo Honesty VII

1877

Mary quickly learned Efik, the language of the villages of the river area near the mission house. She spent her days teaching school to village boys. Some natives wanted their boys to go to school so they could be better traders. Girls were not allowed to attend school. Most natives didn't see the value of school, so they sent their slaves to attend. Mary helped Mammy at the mission house and traveled to the villages on weekends. She spoke to as many villagers as possible, inviting them to Sunday worship and helping with their medical needs during her visits. Mary loved her work, except—she didn't feel like a real missionary.

She lived in a house, not a hut. She ate imported British food, not local food. She was now the schoolteacher but didn't lead the mission work. She wanted to live with the natives, move further into Africa, and be in charge of her own mission station.

Around the supper table, Mary talked with Daddy Anderson. "Is there a mission I could help further inland?"

"Other than David Livingstone, no one's been further than thirty-five miles inland." Daddy Anderson shook his head. "I wouldn't support a move for you. Too much danger. You're a marvelous teacher."

"Yes, she is," Mrs. Anderson winked at Mary, "if you can keep her from climbing trees or running races with her students." She smiled at Mary as she passed another biscuit to her.

Several months after Mary arrived in Calabar, a Christian chief named King Eyo Honesty invited her to visit. King Eyo had been converted to Christianity as a boy by Hope Waddell, the founder of the Calabar Mission. King Eyo was the high chief of Creek Town. Many of the Africans had adopted some of the British ways and used the title *king*, instead of *chief*. Mary traveled by canoe early in the morning to attend Eyo's church. Mary wondered if King Eyo would help her find a way to visit the inland villages. After church, a servant led Mary along the path to Eyo's palace. Mary smiled at the children chasing each other and giggled when the children squealed before running away. Wherever Mary went, she was getting used to children's reactions to her ivory skin and red hair.

Eyo's palace reminded Mary of a European home. It was a two-story wooden house with open porches in the front. When they arrived at the palace, the servant announced, "King Eyo Honesty the Seventh," and bowed.

Mary curtsied. King Eyo didn't wear a native tunic. He was dressed like an Englishman in gray pinstripe trousers, dinner jacket, and top hat. Missing, however, was a shirt, and beads were draped over his bare chest instead.

"Miss Slessor." The king sat at the head of a large table. He gestured for Mary to sit on a woven mat near him.

Seeing King Eyo barefoot, Mary slipped her feet out of her brown leather shoes before she sat. "I am happy to meet you, King Eyo, but I'm afraid I've scared the children."

"They say your hair is on fire." King Eyo's deep bass voice boomed as he laughed.

Mary patted her head. "My hair drew attention even in Scotland."

"Your hair matches our dazzling sunsets."

"King Eyo, you speak perfect English."

"I learned English as a boy from missionaries."

Attendants set a platter of steaming food in front of her.

"My cook prepared roasted goat, yams, fish soup." King Eyo motioned for Mary to begin.

A woman servant with a water pitcher stood next to Mary and pointed to her hands. Mary hesitated and then held out her hands over an empty bowl as the servant poured water over them. Then she pressed a towel into Mary's palms to blot them dry.

Mary loved the taste of the local foods, compared to the imported canned food she ate at the mission. During dinner, King Eyo and Mary shared their background, their conversion to Christianity, and the stories of their families.

"Your mother survived much loss and now gave you up to be a missionary."

Mary looked off for a moment and then focused again on King Eyo. "Her strength comes from God." Mary said and smiled. "She read every article about you in the *Missionary Record.*"

King Eyo wiped the sweat beading across his forehead. "How impressed I am that people across the ocean would be interested in our country. I'd like to write to your mother."

Mary clasped her hands. "Mother would love that." She looked into King Eyo's eyes. "Creek Town is clean and well-run. The Duke Town missionaries say you are an honorable leader. I understand why."

"I credit God." Eyo furrowed his brow. "Life in the Calabar region is harsh. There is no trust among the tribes. Customs are hard to change."

Mary stopped eating. "King Eyo, I want to teach everyone about Christ's love. More than anything, I want to teach the inland people about Christ's love."

Eyo stiffened. "Evil is practiced there. Inland is far too dangerous for a white woman."

Mary crossed her arms. "There's so much opposition—Daddy Anderson, the mission board, and now—you."

Eyo shook his head. "Moving is sure death for you."

"I had hoped you would help." Mary blinked back tears. "But thank you for considering my safety."

"Miss Slessor," Eyo paused. "Do not be in such a hurry. Our ways here in Africa are slower. Isn't the God we love a God of patience?"

Mary nodded. "Yes, Jesus never hurried."

"You have ambitious plans." King Eyo peeled an orange.

"I feel trapped. I'm so close to the people who've never heard of Jesus but I'm unable to reach them. When will God open a way?"

"I must impress upon you the native ways haven't changed here in hundreds of years. You must wait. The African bush is not safe."

Mary returned to Duke Town and continued her duties. She had been in Africa for almost three years and felt thankful she had never come down with malaria, a fever and fatigue that lingered for months and often killed missionaries.

One day in June, in the middle of the rainy season, Mary staggered into the mission house, soaked to the skin, after spending a day in the villages.

Mammy Anderson rushed to Mary's side, cupping her arm around her shoulder, and helped her sit. "Mary, you've got a fever."

"Mother . . . ?" Everything looked fuzzy. Oh, how she missed her mother. "Mother, is that you?"

Mary's teeth chattered. She was freezing. Her head was spinning and she . . . couldn't . . . hold . . . her . . . head . . .

Trying to remember where she was, Mary opened her eyes.

Mammy Anderson held her hand. "Oh, child. I'm so glad to see your eyes. I haven't left your side for three days." Mammy Anderson propped Mary's head up and gave her a sip of water.

Mary moaned. She felt *so* tired.

"The doctor examined you while you were unconscious. You have malaria."

Mary tried to comprehend everything Mammy said.

"We're sending you home. I've already booked your passage on the next steamer." Mammy Anderson patted Mary's hand.

Going home to Scotland? She was supposed to be in Africa one more year before her furlough. Was she finished being a missionary? A lone tear trickled down her cheek.

"If you don't rest, dear, you'll die."

After three years in Africa, Mary left Calabar on June 22, 1879, and rested the entire voyage. Even after arriving in Scotland, she could only take a few steps without stopping. But after months of rest and her mother's and sisters' tender care, her health improved.

The mission board expected her to speak to churches now that she was well, but public speaking made her nervous. As hard as it was for her to stand in front of a crowd, she did it for the cause of Jesus. Over the next year, she spoke in hundreds of churches around Scotland.

She shared stories about her friend, King Eyo, and the boys who were learning to read the Bible. She told how most African natives are slaves, branded like animals, sold or killed at the whim of the owner. She explained the practice of witchcraft among the villages. She told them how twins were believed to be evil, killed at birth, and the mother banished to live in the bush. People flocked to hear Mary.

She encouraged them. "We need more missionaries. And when God prompts you to pray for a missionary, pray. You never know what danger the missionary could be in."

Mary had been home for fourteen months. Healthy, invigorated, and healed from the malaria, she traveled back to Duke Town in September, 1880. Mary had big plans. She wanted to go back and save the orphaned children. She wanted to stop the killing of twins. She wanted to help the women. And she wanted to have a mission station of her own. She prayed and wondered if God would send her where she wanted to go—deep into the African bush.

7

A New Town

1880

The first night in Duke Town, Mary pushed the boiled beef on her plate to the side. She missed her family, but she felt so happy to be back in Africa. While in Scotland, she'd written the mission board and requested a mission station further inland.

Daddy Anderson cleared his throat like he did when he had something important to say. "You speak Efik as well as I do. You know how to nurse, teach, and preach. I think you're ready to manage a mission. The board approved. You'll be in charge of the Old Town mission."

Mary felt as happy as the day her foot stepped across the gangplank onto the *Ethiopia*. She leaned forward. "I'm ready."

Her eyes scanned the shelf of tinned food the missionaries bought from the ships. Instead of spending money to pay for the imported food, she could eat the native foods, send her paycheck home, and get her mother out of that cramped apartment.

"Mary." He looked straight into her eyes. "We have fifteen men missionaries working here in Duke Town. You'll be the only white woman in Old Town."

Mammy Anderson picked up Mary's plate. "Twenty-five years ago in Old Town, Chief Willy ordered his wives, children, and slaves to be killed when he died. His eldest son killed all of them. Then the British retaliated. The missionaries didn't support this bloodshed on either side, but ever since, Old Town hasn't liked foreigners."

Daddy Anderson continued. "Since then, missionaries haven't survived in Old Town long." He shook his head. "There hasn't been a missionary there in over two years. I don't know what you'll find. One final warning," Daddy Anderson said. "Old Town is not a safe place for a woman to work alone."

"I have to go where my Master needs me," Mary said.

"God be with you, dear."

The next day, Mary arranged a paddle crew. She stepped into the canoe, as she had done so many times before, but this time the ride felt different. Her heart pumped with excitement. The men paddled the canoe, skirting around the crocodiles. As they approached Old Town, the canoe slowed to a stop. The hull amplified the sound as the canoe scraped across the sand. A tall pole stood at the top of a hill at the entrance to Old Town.

Clunk, clunk, clunk.

Mary shielded her eyes from the bright sun and studied the hillside. A skull dangled at the top of a pole. Its hollow thud sounded as the wind rattled the skull against the pole. *Stay away, stay away* was the rhythm it spoke.

"That's a warning, Miss Slessor." The crew leader pointed to the skull.

Mary's stomach knotted up. Fear? Excitement? *Lord, surely You wouldn't bring me so far from home to be killed, would You?* Mary looked at the crew leader. "I have to trust God. He saved David against Goliath. Old Town is my home now."

The sweat gleamed on each crew member's black skin as they silently unloaded her trunks, glancing back at the skull the whole time.

Mary prayed as they tramped through the forest. The jungle's *chiff-chiff* and *whirr-whirr* of a thousand different bugs and birds sounded like a huge orchestra. Sparrows flitted from branch to branch, and spiny lizards jumped from bush to bush. The vines snaked around huge tree trunks.

Mary sniffed the musk-scented forest. She loved the different shades from black green to shiny, bright green. Even though she knew walking through the jungle was dangerous, the trees' canopy made her feel safe and serene. The group carried her trunks up the hill, down a ravine, and over the jungle path until they found the old mission.

At the sight of the hut, Mary gasped. The mud hut's thatched roof leaned. Plants had overtaken the yard. *God, I need to be safe. This hut won't protect me from a mosquito.*

The paddlers hacked through the vines and bushes in the yard, so they could look inside the hut. Leaves and limbs carpeted the floor. A rat scurried past. The crew leader held a molted snakeskin between his fingers.

Mary turned to the skittish crew, assigned clean-up chores, and worked alongside them to clean the hut. Most villages swarmed with visitors, but no one was in sight here.

The crew carried limbs, leaves, and mounds of dirt out of the hut. Others cut away the thick bushes and plants that had grown over the mission yard. They used dried gourds or calabashes as bowls and swished the hut's floor clean. They carried drinking water from the river and set Mary's trunks, which held all her cooking pots and other supplies, inside the hut.

As she said goodbye to the paddle crew, Mary thought about the polished floors, the large windows, and the beautiful mahogany doors at the Duke Town mission house. She took a deep breath and wondered if she should go back with the crew to Duke Town.

A limb cracked. Mary froze for a second. The bushes rustled. Mary clapped her hands in the air, hoping to scare whatever . . . whoever . . . was there.

Was it too late to catch up with the crew before they reached the canoe?

A lizard darted across the yard. Above the *whir* of the insects, Mary could hear the bushes rattle again. Her heart beat like the wild thump of native drums. She was isolated. Alone. Scared. Daddy Anderson's words haunted her, "You'll be in a wicked area *alone*."

Stay with me, Lord. Keep me safe. She scanned the yard and the forest's edge. Suddenly, a monkey screeched, scampered down a tree, and scurried into the forest.

Mary rushed inside the hut and slumped against the mud wall. Her heart pounded. Sweat dripped from her forehead and her throat felt dry. She laughed at herself. "I'm afraid of a monkey." She shuffled through her trunk and opened her Bible and let the words of Isaiah soothe her, "Fear not, for I am with thee."

Medicine bag and Bible in one hand and machete in the other, she followed the path to Old Town. From the direction of the village, Mary could see the gray smoke from the cooking fires curling into the air. The smell of the smoke mingled with animal odors. Flies and mosquitoes swarmed over animal waste and discarded food thrown in pits near the path. Slaves scurried past as Mary made her way through the village looking for the chief. Mary saw children chasing goats and dogs over the dirt paths throughout the village. When they caught sight of her, some followed her, some tried to touch her arm, and others hid.

When she reached the chief's hut, the guards pointed their spears at her. The chief ordered his guards to lower their spears and invited Mary to sit with him.

Mary spoke in Efik to the chief. "I have come to live in the mission house and help your people."

"I've heard of the white woman from the village drums," the chief said. "You have magic powers?"

"No, Chief. I don't have magic, but I serve God, who is all powerful. I want to begin a school and church in Old Town and teach your people about God's power."

Then the chief pushed forward a woman with an oozing infection on her arm. "The witch doctors failed."

Mary applied disinfectant and a poultice to the wound where she recognized human teeth marks. She saw evidence of other bites from rats and snakes on others in the tribe. The remainder of the afternoon, Mary talked with the chief. She asked the chief for a woman to help her in her yard. Several times the guards chased away the curious people who leaned closer and closer to see Mary.

The chief listened to her Bible stories. Before nightfall, he finally answered, "I wondered if the God-woman would come."

Mary's heart soared. If she'd given in to her fear, she would have missed the job God had sent her to do. *God, thank You for going before me and preparing the way.*

Back in her hut, Mary fell to her knees and prayed. *Lord, help me help them. They need a hospital or at least a doctor. They need You. Will You help me free the Old Town people of their old customs?*

Sweat poured down her neck and back. She tugged at the tight collar around her neck and flapped her long skirt to cool off. Her hair, which had fallen from her bun, now cascaded down her back and clung to her sweat-drenched shirt. The setting sun seeped through the gaps in the roof and cast shadows across her trunk. The hinges on the trunk creaked as she lifted the lid to find a lantern.

Mary removed the lantern's globe, adjusted the wick, lit it, and then grabbed the scissors. With a mirror positioned between her knees, she began to cut. *Snip, snip, snip.* Her long hair fell into a pile.

With her newly cropped hair, she read her Bible and sipped tea. The Old Town villagers hadn't killed her. *Thank You, God.* How could she help the women and teach them not to fear twins or their mothers? How could she help a village understand twins weren't tragedies but blessings? She couldn't. But with God's help, nothing was impossible.

8

Forest Fashion

The chief sent a woman named Asani to help Mary. During their first few weeks, Mary taught Asani Scottish hymns and told her Bible stories. Asani took care of the cleaning and swept the daily shedding of leaves from the cluster of trees around Mary's yard. Asani also helped cook.

The Old Town village and nearby villages, Qua, Akim, and Ikot Ansa, had a weekly market day. Asani showed Mary the market. Neat piles of cassava, plantains, bananas, yams, fish, and baskets of beans lay on blankets on the ground as swarms of people carried baskets of shells, beads, or brass rods to trade. She saw liquor bottles for trade and was disappointed to learn the only thing the river villages traded with the other villages was guns and alcohol.

Mary traded with cloth and brass rods. Or she used the beads and shells the villagers sometimes gave her. Asani prepared the fresh foods they bought at the market. Mary was eating just like the natives. She was able to save money by eating local foods, and she sent part of her missionary salary to her mother. The only luxury Mary spent money on was her tea, a Scottish custom she wouldn't give up.

Early one misty morning, Mary rose to warm tea water on the fire and nearly stumbled over a large, green bundle of leaves at her door.

Mary pulled the leaves back. "A baby!"

"Asani, someone's left a baby here."

"They trust you—you are a God-woman. A slave mother probably died, and no one else will care for the child." Asani shrugged. "Slave children are usually buried with the mother. Everyone has too many children to care for an orphan."

Oh, God help me teach the people the value of human life. "This baby isn't going to die if I can help it." Mary heated tea, then dipped her finger in the tea, and let the baby suck it off her finger. Then she layered a wooden box with large leaves and old newspapers sent to her from Scotland. "The box will have to be your crib, wee one."

During the next year, Mary gave a home to three sets of twins to prevent their deaths. She brought outcast women to live and work with her. The crowded hut didn't feel like a sacrifice at all to Mary when it meant saving a life.

One evening near dark, Mary heard beating drums and singing men. Beyond her fenced yard, she could see native men wearing hats with large feathers hanging from them or animals masks with horns. They were the Egbo runners, a secret society of free men who enforced laws. The Egbo runner announced, "Anyone who murders twins will be hung."

Thank you, God. Mary cried tears of joy at the news.

Mary taught school. After several months of teaching, helping the sick, and sharing the story of Jesus in Old Town, people began to trust her. They even started bringing their disputes to her. Many accepted Jesus as their Savior. Even the chief asked Mary to meet with him. "I am banishing our god, Abasi. Our laws aren't following God's laws." The villagers grew to love Mary and called her Ma—a title of great honor.

By 1882, Mary had been in Old Town for two years and realized how much she missed the companionship of others. Here in the forest, surrounded by thousands, she still felt lonely and longed for conversation with friends. She arranged to go to Duke Town for a few days to find help to build an orphanage for the abandoned children.

Her heart raced at the thought of seeing her friends again.

But at Duke Town, the house was unusually silent. Mary walked through the house; everything was in order the way Mammy Anderson kept it.

Miss Fuller stood in the kitchen. "I'm sorry, dear. Since you last visited, Mrs. Sutherland died. Fevers. Malaria. The house is so quiet . . ." Miss Fuller began to cry. "Now Mammy Anderson is sick."

Daddy Anderson and Mary nursed Mammy Anderson, but she died within a few days. Brokenhearted, Mary threw herself onto her cot and wailed. Dear Mrs. Sutherland and Mammy Anderson had been like mothers to her. Instead of a rest, she'd arrived for a funeral. Maybe Africa really was the white man's grave.

In late 1882, shortly after Mary returned to Old Town, two foreign mission deputies from Scotland came to visit. When they arrived from Duke Town early on a Sunday morning, Mary and two boys led the visitors as she began her Sunday travel routine for church services. She visited the farms on the way into each village. The farms were fields of vegetable gardens in open land away from the bush, sometimes with a few huts near the fields.

The boys rang a bell hung on the end of a long pole to alert people for Sabbath school. Mary and her guests visited Qua first, and then trekked to Akim, Ikot Ansa, then home to Old Town. When the group returned to Old Town in the afternoon, Mary held Sabbath school again.

"You're a whirlwind, Miss Slessor," the deputy said.

The other gentleman wiped the sweat off his forehead. "You covered miles of territory in this heat."

"God's power keeps me moving. It's exhilarating to see so many Christians," Mary said, "but the new Christians often go right back into their old customs when there's a problem."

"How many converts are there?"

"It's difficult to keep a count. Hundreds come to church services, but not all who come to worship have committed to Christ. The customs here are slowly changing. People are beginning to trust me, and some have accepted Jesus." Mary pointed to the huts. "I am encouraged when I see the natives' heathen habits changing. As you can see, many of the clay idols which used to adorn the front of each hut have disappeared."

Even though Mary had traveled all day, she preached again for the Sunday evening service. Just like Mammy Anderson had taught her, she arranged a table with a white cloth, her Bible, and a lantern under the palm trees. "This is the biggest meeting of the week," Mary told the visitors.

It looked like everyone from the village had gathered for the evening service. The men sat on skins or mats at the front, women sat behind, and slaves stood in the back. Mary opened her Bible to the fifth chapter of John and spoke to the natives in Efik. "'Verily, verily, I say unto you, He that heareth my word, and believeth on him that sent me, hath everlasting life, and shall not come into condemnation; but is passed from death unto life.' Our Savior pardons and heals. Won't you be made whole in Christ?"

Villagers waited after the service to talk, asking questions about her God, and some asked to be "a God-man like you're are a God-woman." The stars twinkled overhead, as a small group of natives walked Mary back to her hut. "Tie-suno, Ma Akamba."

"You rest softly, too, my dear brothers and sisters."

Nearly three years passed in Old Town. Some behaviors changed. The Egbo runners had announced the new law—death for anyone who killed twins. Yet Mary knew the natives were still killing twins but in secret. The mother, father, or another relative would shove the twins through a hole in the back of the hut for animals to kill. She talked to the new Christians and asked them for help. "Will you alert me as soon as twins are born?"

Late every night, Mary kneeled and prayed. With God's help, she hoped one day she could convince the people that twins were not from an evil spirit. With the rescued children asleep around her, Mary opened her Bible to Psalms. "Bless the Lord, O my soul; and forget not all his benefits."

A thump sounded outside. "Run, Ma, run!"

"Oh, God, help me to get there," Mary prayed. Her bare feet pounded against the dirt path. "Get me there in time, Lord."

A crowd had gathered. Word traveled fast in villages. Arms waving frantically through the air, Mary screamed, "Get out of the way," hoping the noise would scare the people. She pushed past the women in the hut. No babies.

She ran to the back of the hut and found the twins lying on the ground below a hole in the hut. *Alive.* Mary gathered the babies in her arms and ran. She didn't dare look back to see if anyone followed her. As her foot crossed into the mission yard, she whispered, "Thank You, God."

Gently, she wiped each baby clean. Tiny cries erupted. "Hush now, sweet child." Mary slid a finger into the girl's tiny hand. "This reminds me of holding my baby sister, Janie, when she was born."

Mary looked at the scrawny little babies in her arms. "Wee girl, you will be Janie. And, young man, you shall be Robert." Mary spooned tea in each squalling baby's mouth. "Lord, please don't let the babies die."

9
A Canoe for a Queen
1883

The twins lived, and Mary's hut teemed with children. But Mary had a new problem. Chief Okon of Ibaka had sent an invitation for her to come tell his village about the white man's God. Mary was thrilled by the opportunity, but the Old Town natives weren't. They were sure she would be harmed. Mary sent a messenger to Duke Town requesting a canoe and paddlers to take her to Ibaka.

King Eyo heard about Mary's plans, but instead of a canoe from Duke Town, he sent a runner with a message for Mary. Dressed in a red tunic and cap, the runner announced the message from King Eyo. "Ibaka is lawless and ruthless. This invitation is a trick. They'll take you captive and kill you."

Mary smiled at Eyo's messenger. "Tell dear King Eyo that God is greater than man."

The runner returned the next day. "King Eyo will send a royal canoe and paddlers for the trip. You are our Ma and must not arrive in Ibaka looking like a nameless stranger. You will travel like a queen."

Mary made arrangements for the children living with her to stay with other Christians in the village. She would take the four oldest children with her to Ibaka for a two-week visit.

On the designated day, a few weeks later, King Eyo's bright yellow-and-red canoe arrived at dusk although Mary had been waiting for it since early morning. In the pouring rain, about a hundred villagers stood along the path to the river, watching the paddlers collect supplies. Mary walked the muddy path to the river. Slaves, hidden in the bushes, reached their brown arms out to touch Mary as she passed.

"We will take revenge on anyone who hurts you, Ma."

My sweet friends. How I love them, Mary thought.

"They better be good to our Mother."

Mary hesitated for a moment. Maybe King Eyo was right.

The setting sun and the stormy sky darkened the path. The mud churned under her feet. As Mary led her four oldest children, one gasped and pointed toward the canoe. "Ma, it's so big!"

Reed torches lit the scene. A long canoe with a shade canopy swayed at the water's edge.

The lead canoe man stepped forward. "Forty foot long. Thirty-three paddlers. King Eyo sent the best for you, Ma." The paddlers heaved eight large bags of rice into the canoe; these were a gift for the chief from Mary. Then they helped the children into the canoe.

The sky had turned black. Three drummers thumped a beat and the command was given to set off. "Sio uden!"

Mary held her head back and listened to the deep voices of the thirty-three paddlers singing a beat as they rowed and the drummer drummed. "Ho. Ho. Ho. We are honored. Ho. Ho. We have our Ma. On we go. Ho. Ho. Ho. Into the night."

The night noises of the jungle filled the air, water striders skimmed the river's surface, and lightning bugs blinked in the distant forest as the canoe glided across the dark waters. Mary closed her eyes and listened. She'd been dying to serve God in Africa all her life, and that's all that mattered, even if she died serving.

The sunrise gleamed golden across the river. Elephants trumpeted in the distance. Two paddlers ran to Mary's side, clasping their hands together as a seat.

Mary shook her head. "I'll walk."

"No, Ma. King Eyo's orders. The people must know you are our White Ma. We will take you to Chief Okon and then return in two weeks to return you to Old Town."

In the distance, Mary could see the fields where elephants had traveled. The trip to Chief Okon's hut reminded Mary of her first visits to other villages as the natives scurried into the woods. She knew none of them had seen a white woman before.

Guards with painted faces and tall spears stood next to the chief's hut. The paddlers set the rice in front of Chief Okon, and the two men lowered Mary to the ground. Her children stood behind her. She pointed to the rice and spoke in Efik. "A gift for you."

Chief Okon nodded approval. "News of you and your God spreads among the villages. Teach me book."

Mary sent the paddlers back to their canoe to return to King Eyo. Then she unwrapped a leather pouch and opened the thin pages of her Bible. "He is your God too. The Bible is everyone's book. Let me read to you." Mary flipped the pages and began to read, "'He that heareth my word, and believeth on him that sent me, hath everlasting life . . .'"

"Live forever?"

"We can live forever in heaven. God asks only that we believe in Him."

Chief Okon motioned for Mary to sit, and Mary sent her children to play. A slave set a platter of herbs and fish in front of them. Okon waved a hand over the food. "We rely on fish. The elephants have destroyed our farms."

"I saw the trampled fields."

Chief Okon held an elephant tusk in front of Mary. "We used to hunt elephants, but it takes many days and is dangerous."

He pointed to a gash on a slave's arm. "Can you fix?"

In Okon's yard, surrounded by Okon and other curious members of his household, Mary bandaged the cut. Soon others asked for help with different injuries and ailments until the line formed out of the hut. For hours, Mary spoke of Jesus, the Great Healer, and prayed with each person as she dispensed more bandages and medicine.

"Chief!" A man ran toward the hut. "Boa constrictor."

"Prepare a hunt."

The village became a flurry of noise as guards shouted directions. A band of men painted with thick white stripes across their faces and chests, carried guns, clubs, and cutlasses and disappeared into the jungle.

The men carried the dead boa into the village, threw it into a sack, and took it into the chief's hut.

At nightfall, Chief Okon led Mary to his hut. "My honored guest will have my room to sleep."

Skulls, wood carvings, and food offerings lined the outside of the hut. Mary jumped as she tried to stifle a scream, "Remove the snake—please."

Chief Okon smiled. "Good pillow."

"No, no, Chief Okon." She didn't want to offend him, but she couldn't sleep with a snake. "I-I don't use pillows."

Chief Okon grabbed the sack and carried it out.

Outside, the village children poked their heads through the window slits. Mary sang her children to sleep and then found a blanket to hang while she prepared herself for bed. Two of Okon's wives shuffled in. A strong mixture of sweat and coconut oil scented the air.

"We will keep you from being lonely."

Mary wondered how she could possibly be lonely, but she knew the tradition. The people considered sleeping in the chief's hut a great honor, and they would never leave a guest alone. Mary's children slept on woven mats nearby. Both wives, on either side of her snored into her ears, and her tiny frame was squashed between them.

The African air was hot. Sweat dribbled off her forehead. The crowded hut had no ventilation. Lizards scurried across the roof sending showers of dirt onto her face. A rat ran through the hut. Sleeping was impossible, so she waited for sunrise.

The next day, people from other villages gathered to hear. Mary stood on a box to project her voice to teach the Bible lesson. Mary opened her Bible and began. "In God's book is the old, old story—the story of God's love for you." In the afternoon, sick and injured people lined up for the white woman's medicine. As she always did, Mary told each sick and injured person about God, the healer of wounds and wounded hearts.

Each night, the chief's wives came to the hut, and Mary hardly slept. By the sixth night, Mary had adjusted to the hut's conditions and was fatigued enough to sleep soundly. But later in the night a crash of thunder woke her. Lightning scrawled across the sky.

Her children screamed. The wind sounded like a train to Mary. She'd never witnessed such a fierce storm and realized that this storm was a tornado. Mary pulled her children close, and then a gust swept the roof off the hut. Rain and hail pelted them. Soaked and shivering, Mary was now happy to huddle together with the wives and her children for warmth.

She tried to soothe her children's fears. "We'll sing our favorite songs, and soon the storm will be over."

When the tornado finally passed, their voices were hoarse from singing and screaming.

Mary's hands shook as she fumbled through boxes for her children's dry clothes. Her fingers felt icy, her teeth chattered, and her bones ached. She spooned herself a dose of medicine. She felt feverish and weak. It felt just like malaria.

10

Tornado Damage

A clear sky dawned as everyone milled around the village, looking at the damage. Mary struggled to walk. Everything had been tossed around. Canoes were smashed into splinters. The skulls and carved wooden idols that had decorated the huts were scattered across the yards. Mary's children joined the native children, who climbed atop a gigantic kapok tree uprooted by the storm.

Mary caught bits of conversations from a group of women. Their words had nothing to do with the storm.

"Hole in the fence."

"Escape."

"Palaver."

Palaver! Mary knew that meant long meetings, and meetings meant judgment, and judgment meant death. Frantic, she found a couple of whispering women. "What is going on?"

"The storm blew a hole in the wives' fence. Two of the chief's new wives left to visit another young man. They will be punished."

Mary prayed for help. *Oh, God, help me. I am a stranger to these people.* She couldn't barge into a men-only meeting so she paced and prayed. *The wives are young girls, Lord. Only You can save them.*

An hour later, Chief Okon stepped outside to the waiting crowd. "One hundred lashes each."

Mary knew no one could survive that many lashes. "Please, Chief Okon. A hundred lashes with a whip will cut the girls to bits. The lashings will kill them."

Chief Okon ignored Mary and walked toward his hut.

Mary ran behind Okon. "You asked me here to learn about God. This is not His way."

Chief Okon stopped and crossed his arms.

Mary crossed her arms. "Call another palaver." She demanded to attend the meeting. Would the chief drag her to the palaver hut next and punish her?

Okon turned and motioned for Mary to follow. "You wanted a palaver."

Mary couldn't believe Chief Okon was allowing her to speak to the palaver. Her boldness had helped. She prayed silently, cleared her throat, and turned to the girls, who had been brought into the palaver to hear. "You young ladies have brought shame on your husband's house."

The girls' eyes widened.

The men's faces changed from dark, sullen expressions to whoops and hollers of agreement. "The girls are guilty and must be lashed."

Then Mary turned to the men, but they wouldn't stop jeering. Chief Okon pounded a tall pole against the ground. "Quiet!"

Mary made sure she spoke in a calm voice, but she wanted to scream in their faces. She prayed God would soften Okon's heart as she spoke. "You're confining young girls. It's a shame and a blot on your manhood. Our Savior taught us to show mercy." Mary remembered the story in John when Jesus confronted the Pharisees. "Who here is without sin?"

The men waved their hands and yelled.

Mary was too angry to stop now. She yelled back. "You have thirty wives!"

For an hour the men argued until Chief Okon stomped his foot to quiet the men and turned to Mary. "As our guest and our mother, we must listen." The room fell silent as he spoke. "Ten lashings."

Thank You, Jesus, for saving the girls' lives! Mary knew ten lashings would give the girls severe cuts. "Send the girls to me as soon as the punishment is completed. Thank you, gentlemen."

Mary gathered her bandages and medicine. Each movement for her was slow and painful. She still felt feverish, but she kept pushing herself. She had to help the girls. *Please, Lord, help them survive the whipping.* With each crack of the whip, each scream, she cringed. *One, two . . . will they honor their word, Lord? Eight . . . nine . . .ten.*

Several older women carried the bleeding girls to Mary. The barbaric custom broke Mary's heart. She dabbed her tears and washed the deep cuts on the girls' backs. Then she dosed them with laudanum and prayed. Even ten lashes could kill the girls if infection set in or the bleeding didn't stop. *Father, please don't let the girls die.*

Mary taught a few women how to clean and bandage the girls' cuts. Her two-week visit came to an end. The worry that the men would reverse their decision after she had left plagued her. The only thing she could do was pray.

Throngs of people came to tell Mary goodbye as Chief Okon led Mary to the river. "We are honored to have you here. You are the mother of us all. I will escort you back to Creek Town in my canoe."

Okon and his head wife sat on each side of Mary at the helm of the canoe as his oarsmen launched forward. Two hours into their journey the blue sky changed to a greenish gold. Rain began to pelt and lightning lit the sky. Okon shouted commands, but his terrified paddlers ignored all of Okon's commands and screamed instead in fear.

Angry, Mary shouted commands. "Why have you stopped rowing? Move us toward the mangroves or we'll sink." She pointed to the drummer and yelled, "Drum." She turned to the paddlers, "Paddle toward the trees!"

Against the wind and blowing rain, they paddled furiously toward the mangrove trees, tied the canoe to a limb, and climbed into the branches. Mary, Okon, his wife, and Mary's children huddled together in the canoe as another tornado whipped through.

The rain beat down and filled the canoe with water to their knees. Then the storm left as quickly as it had appeared. Mary, Okon, and his wife waited on the river's edge while the paddlers turned the canoe on its side and emptied the water. Then the wet and weary group pushed off again. During the entire ten-hour trip, Mary shivered. The paddlers carried Mary to her hut to the sounds of the Old Town people wailing at the sight of their Ma. "What has happened to our Ma?"

In the hut Mary sat on her cot holding Janie, one of the twins she had rescued. Asani kneeled beside Mary. Tears streamed down Asani's cheeks. "Ma, I am so sorry. A relative came to visit the baby brother while you were away. They took Robert. They . . . tricked . . . me." Asani sobbed. "Baby Robert is dead."

Grieving and feverish, thirty-five-year old Mary stayed bedridden, too weak to sit up. The Old Town people arranged a canoe to take Mary to see a doctor in Duke Town.

"You have malaria again," the doctor said. "You need to go home to Scotland to recuperate."

Mary nodded. "I've made arrangements for the children's care. They are to live with other Christians in Old Town, but I have to take Janie."

"You're too sick to care for a child. Who will take care of the baby if you die on the ship? She's only a few months old."

"She's a twin. Her family will kill her if I leave."

"Mary Slessor—"

"She must go with me."

The doctor placed his hand over Mary's. "Take Janie, but I doubt you'll live."

11

Creek Town

1885

Mary survived the voyage to Scotland and her second bout of malaria. She missed the children who had been living with her in Old Town, but she knew they were living with Christian families. She was thankful to have baby Janie with her.

After months of recovery, she grew accustomed to the foggy, gray-green landscape and the chilly temperature of Scotland again. Her ivory skin and red hair blended in with the locals, but now baby Janie caught the attention of everyone. Mary took Janie with her when she spoke at churches. She saw how people reacted to a black baby and how Janie helped them understand how missionaries saved people's lives. People flocked to hear Mary speak and donated more money to the missions.

The Dundee streets were too busy for Mary. She was more comfortable in Africa. After two years, Mary wanted to go back to Calabar, but her sister Janie had gotten tuberculosis, so Mary delayed her trip. Then Mary's mother caught bronchitis. Mary decided to move her family to a warmer place in England. While she was searching for a house, her other sister, Susan, suddenly died in Dundee. The news was a shock to Mary and her family. No one knew what caused Susan's death. Mary delayed her trip to

Calabar to nurse her mother and sister in their new home in Topsham, England.

Finally, Mrs. Slessor insisted Mary return. "God gave you to me, and I've given you back to Him, my daughter. Africa is where you should be."

Mary felt torn, but she knew her mother was right. Finally, she arranged for someone to care for her mother and sister, and she and baby Janie returned to Africa after a two and a half year furlough.

Janie had left Africa as an infant and didn't remember Africa at all. Mary helped her practice speaking Efik during their voyage. When the ship docked on the Calabar River, Mary welcomed the hot African air. "We're back, Janie, in the place of my dreams."

On December 5, 1885, the ship anchored within sight of Duke Town. Mary and Janie stood on the ship's deck. Janie hid between Mary's legs. "Let go, dear. I can hardly walk. We have to get our land legs back again after a month at sea."

A half-dozen young boys held paddles in a small canoe waiting for passengers. "The boys in the canoe—or you can call it a gig—are going to take us to Duke Town." Mary climbed down the ship's ladder. Janie held her dolly in one hand and clung to a crew member's arm as he carried her down the ladder to the gig.

A boy extended his hand to steady Mary as she stepped in the gig while her trunks were loaded into a different canoe. Minutes later she stepped out of the gig, and Mary was tempted to throw off her boots and feel the African dirt between her toes.

Mary had been assigned to work in King Eyo's village, Creek Town. The mission board had assigned both native workers and missionaries from Duke Town to manage the Old Town mission. She looked down at three-year-old Janie and wondered if her family might still try to kill her. Hopefully, Creek Town was a safe distance away from Janie's family. But Creek Town wasn't inland, and she didn't plan to give up her request to the mission board to work inland. For now, her plans could wait. Mary hoped to prove to the natives that twins weren't evil. Janie was living proof. Even though the Egbo law protected twins, she knew the natives continued to practice twin birth killing in secret.

One day a letter from King Eyo Honesty arrived for Mary in Duke Town by messenger. A few days later, a canoe arrived for Mary and Janie, and soon they were climbing the knoll to Eyo's house. *Boom. Boom. Boom.* Janie plugged her ears.

"The cannon is announcing that King Eyo is ready for visitors." Mary smiled at Janie. "I thought it was loud the first time I visited too."

Along the path to Eyo's house, children played with sticks and chased each other until they spotted Mary. Then the children hid.

Mary broke a large bean pod from a tree and showed Janie how to open the pod. "Here, lassie. We'll practice counting the beans later."

Mary noticed changes in Calabar and Creek Town. More British ships. More British officers. More European-style buildings. *Everything has changed, even me. Now I'm an experienced missionary*, she thought.

A servant led Mary and Janie to King Eyo, who sat in an ornately carved wooden chair. He tipped his hat like an English gentleman. "Miss Mary Slessor."

Mary curtsied. Janie tightened her grip on Mary's hand. "King Eyo, this is my daughter Janie. She thinks she's Scottish," Mary laughed. "But she's learning Efik quickly."

Janie clung to Mary's long skirt.

"Welcome back to Creek Town. How is your mother?"

Mary felt a sharp pang, remembering how pale her mother had looked before she left. "Sick. I wonder if I made a mistake. Should I go back to care for my family?"

"Your heart is torn?"

Mary nodded yes.

"Mary, your mother sent you back because she is committed to your mission work."

"Yes, Mother understands how important missionaries are." Mary paused. "Yet the feeling that I'll never see her again won't go away."

Over the next few days, Mary spent hours swinging on a hammock, reading, and picking bouquets of flowers with Janie. Every morning and evening, Mary and King Eyo studied the Bible together.

King Eyo discussed the political situation with Mary. "You understand the British law better than I. The British want to open up more trade routes. I support trading, but not by force. The inland tribes will fight."

"I agree." Mary nodded. "We must ask the British to wait for the missions to contact the inland tribes first."

"I value your advice about my relationship with the British. They plan to build roads next, and I plan to cooperate. You are a queen, Mary. Our white queen."

How could I be called a queen? "I am God's servant and will do as He leads."

Soon after her visit with King Eyo, a runner delivered a telegram to Mary. Her mother had died December 31. In March another telegram came saying that her sister Janie had died. Mary continued her duties but spent the evenings crying over their loss. With no family left to worry about her, Mary's desire grew to serve further inland.

But Mary's African family also grew. She had saved several children who were sick or abandoned, and she saved some who were twins. Not all of these children stayed with her permanently. Some of the children were adopted by

Christian Africans or were raised by other missionaries. Others returned to their families after Mary had nursed sick ones to health. The mission compound in Creek Town soon filled up—a six-year old girl, and two boys, eight and ten. Mary trained a thirteen-year-old girl, Inyang, to help with household duties so she could teach, preach, and nurse.

One morning, the sun had already dried the dew, and the day promised not only to be hot, but exciting. Mary expected missionaries from Duke Town to arrive soon. She had just finished the morning Bible lesson with the children. As Inyang scurried around with her palm frond brush sweeping, Janie traced figures in the dirt, and Mary started her sewing.

Mary got up from her sewing and checked on a noise coming from the bush. A bare-chested stranger, dressed in a cloth tied to his waist, stood in the flowered path at the edge of her yard, carrying a sack. He wasn't the missionary she expected.

"Hello." Mary waved, but the man didn't move. Mary assumed the man had come for medical attention. "Are you hurt?" Mary asked.

"I just want to look."

"Look?"

"I want to watch her."

"Who?"

"My daughter."

Mary's heart pounded. *Swish, swish, swish* went Inyang's broom. Should she try to hide Janie? Had he come to take her back with him? Mary repeated Bible verses as she walked toward the man. *Give ear to my prayer, O God. Protect Janie.*

The man looked so scared Mary felt sorry for him and reached for his hand. "Come and meet your daughter."

Four-year-old Janie drew circles in the dirt with her stick as Mary led the man toward her. "Hug her."

Janie's father stiffened. Mary knew he was scared be-cause Janie was a twin.

"She's a wee girl. She can't hurt you." Mary smiled and kept a constant prayer going in her head. *Lord, help him understand Janie isn't an evil spirit.*

"Janie," Mary knelt next to her, "this is your father."

The corners of his lips curved up as he squatted on the ground next to Janie. Father and daughter sat side-by-side, swirling shapes in the dirt.

Mary exhaled her breath. If Janie's father believed his twin daughter wasn't evil, there was hope for the entire village. Maybe the people would change their superstitious beliefs.

The man untied the sack, reached in, and showed her a yam as long as a banana. Then he handed Mary the sack. "A gift."

She looked into the man's eyes. Mary could see the sin-cerity in them. "Thank you."

"I must go." He hugged Janie, rose, and then disap-peared into the woods as quietly as he had come.

12

Government Business

1887

During Mary's time in Creek Town, Mary and King Eyo met often. Eyo continued to seek Mary's advice concerning the British.

"Mary, there's a possibility of war between Africa and England. The British plan to bring gunboats to claim territory and open up trade routes with the inland tribes."

"Why fight the Africans?"

"The British want to secure the inland so the natives will follow British law."

"Force is not the way to communicate with the natives."

Eyo nodded. "I agree. We need to teach the British how to work with our people. You understand both cultures. I might arrange a meeting next week with the British representatives."

Mary looked down at her own sunbaked skin. "They won't listen to me. King Eyo, I'm not a diplomat. I eat like an African and think like an African. I'm . . . I'm an African."

"Mary, everyone respects you."

"God uses me for His work. I teach the way God wants us to treat one another." Mary paused. "I love the natives as much as my family."

By 1886, Mary began writing to the mission board for permission to go inland. Mary shared her dreams with

Eyo. "King Eyo, I want to move inland to work with the Okoyong."

Eyo's smile disappeared. "Have the Okoyong sent an invitation?

"No."

King Eyo continued. "They trust no one. Last week the Okoyong killed forty people when a lower chief died. Burying people alive is common. They still practice boiling oil and poison bean trials."

Mary wasn't intimidated by King Eyo's story. "I have no family alive to worry about me now."

King Eyo thumped the table with his hand. "To this day, an unofficial war continues between the coastal tribes and the Okoyong. If you oppose their ways, they'll demand your life."

Mary didn't want to show disrespect to her friend and mentor. Was Creek Town as far as God wanted her to go? *God, You sent me to Africa, and I know You will protect me, even in the darkest region.*

"King Eyo, I've always dreamed of going upcountry to teach the inlanders. In their hearts, they're no different from you and me."

"The mission board must send a man. You are our Eka Kpukpru Owo—the mother of us all."

"Don't the Okoyong deserve to hear God's story of salvation the same as the people on the fringes of Africa?"

King Eyo stood. "They are headhunters. They sleep with their weapons. If you move there, no one will be able to protect you."

Mary prayed for two more years, and by 1888, her prayers were answered. She'd petitioned the mission board to work in Okoyong Territory, and after a long wait, they finally approved her request. Mary arranged for other missionaries to watch her children while she spent a couple of days exploring. King Eyo's attitude softened, and he provided his canoe and paddlers for her again.

Before receiving the mission's approval, she had taken some unsuccessful exploratory trips with other missionaries to meet with the Okoyong. But this day was the only time she had ventured this far into the jungle alone, accompanied only by the boatmen on the canoe. She stopped in a section of Okoyong territory that she'd never visited before and trudged through the paths.

As she neared a village, guards raised their spears and surrounded Mary.

"I come in peace. No weapons." Mary set a basket of yams at her feet and held her hands out, hoping they would understand her actions since the Okoyong spoke Bantu, not Efik.

A warrior, with white lines painted across his arms and chest and wearing a feathered cap on his head, stepped forward. "I am Chief Edem," he said in perfect Efik. "Who is with you?"

"I am alone," Mary said.

The chief snorted. "You are the white Ma the talking drums tell about?"

"Yes, I am Mary Slessor." She prayed silently. *Protect me, Lord. I am wearing Your shield of faith.*

On the other visits, the guards had turned the missionaries away at the river. Mary prayed and waited. Would they kill her?

"Lower your weapons," he directed the men. Chief Edem led Mary to his hut and then motioned Mary to sit on a wooden stool. "Sit."

Edem sat in his chair and his guards surrounded him.

People milled around everywhere. Animals had no boundaries, and dogs, goats, sheep, cows, chickens, and rats mingled between the crowded huts. The odor from the unwashed and sweaty people was so strong it turned her stomach.

A savage-looking crowd formed. Women came covered only in swirls of yellow paint; naked children ran and hid. The men's eyes were fearless, and their faces were covered with an assortment of painted designs. Everyone had piercings and scars.

Chief Edem shaded his eyes from the sun. "You are brave."

Mary had a lump in her throat and almost lost her courage, but she said a silent prayer and then spoke. "I want to live among you." *Please God, let Edem say yes. He's turned back anyone who traveled upriver to Ekenge before.*

Chief Edem gathered his lower chiefs to a palaver to discuss Mary's request.

Mary slept on a bed of sticks that night and waited for their answer. The next morning she woke to gunshots. Two women who'd left their village to get water at a spring had been shot. Mary realized King Eyo's warnings were right and thanked God for protecting her.

Chief Edem found Mary and shared the decision. "We want to learn book."

Mary's heart felt like it would soar—knowing God would change lives. She held her Bible for them to see. "This book is the oldest story in the world. Jesus came from heaven to die to save us from our sins." Encouraged, she continued. "I'll need land for a school, church, and my hut."

Chief Edem grunted. "You don't need land. There are plenty of huts."

Mary continued. "If you want to learn book, I'll need a school."

Chief Edem crossed his arms.

Mary was determined. "My land must be a safe-haven. If someone from your tribe is in my yard, they are not under your rule. They're under God's rule. Will you promise, Chief Edem?"

"Humph." Chief Edem looked at Mary. "A white woman in a village is good. You have medicines. You can trade. A white woman is powerful." He nodded. "Agree."

Mary opened a box and held up a white cone.

The crowd murmured.

Mary poked it with a stick until pieces broke into dust. She dipped her finger and licked the white powder. "Sugar. Taste." Mary held the sugar for the chief.

Chief Edem followed Mary's lead and tasted. He moved his tongue like the sugar had stuck to the roof of his mouth and then flashed a huge smile and dipped his finger again. "Oo-ooh. Sugar sweet too much." All afternoon everyone crowded around Mary to taste the too-sweet-sugar.

Before the evening meal, a native showed Mary some uncooked fur-covered meat. "Cat? Dog? Monkey?" Mary asked. Not wishing to offend, she didn't refuse her meal but wished she were eating the canned meat served in Duke Town.

The sun dipped behind the horizon. Under a canopy of stars, Mary curled up on a bed of muddy sticks covered with corn shucks with three women and an infant beside her. As the big dipper moved across the sky, Mary prayed. The trip had been successful, but what about King Eyo's warning? She was here to teach God's love and His ways. If she opposed their ways, would they kill her? She prayed, *Thy will be done, Lord.*

As soon as she could arrange it, she would move to Ekenge in Okoyong territory—the inland. She needed one more promise. Mary returned to Creek Town, and visited King Eyo right away.

Not sure how he would react, she prayed for God to work on King Eyo's heart. She had the permission of the

mission board, but she wanted Eyo's blessing. He had become like a brother to her.

Eyo invited Mary to sit on his veranda with him. He listened quietly while Mary described every detail of her visit to Okoyong territory. "I counted at least fifty dogs. They barked and chased each other around the huts all night."

"If I didn't believe in God's power, I would never believe you walked into an Okoyong village alone and unarmed. The Okoyong stalk and capture strangers in their territory to sell them to cannibals or as slaves to another tribe."

"I nearly lost my courage, but God armed me." Mary paused. "King Eyo, I have the mission board's approval. May I have your blessing?"

King Eyo smiled. "Who am I to interfere with God's work?"

13

The Okoyong in Ekenge

August 1888

The rain smacked against the river's surface. Men hauled Mary's trunks to the river as a crowd gathered along the path. In spite of slipping in the mud and listening to the wailing of the Creek Town villagers, Mary made her way to the canoe. She huddled under the canoe's palm-leaf canopy with her three boys, six-year-old Janie, and a newly adopted baby Annie. Across from her sat another missionary, Mr. Bishop, who was a last-minute volunteer.

"You're a gentleman to offer, Mr. Bishop."

"My heart wrenched to see you alone with five children, bound for unknown territory."

The wind blew against the canoe and slowed their journey. In spite of the weather, the paddlers sang the entire trip—a trip that took all day, instead of a few hours. Night began to descend as the canoe arrived.

"We have a three-mile hike to the Ekenge village, Mr. Bishop. If you'll stay behind and unload the rest of the canoe with the paddlers, I'll go ahead to the village to get the children settled."

"Miss Slessor, I came to help you."

"I've traveled this path before." Mary didn't confess she'd never traveled at night in Okoyong territory. "Bring the boxes of dry clothing and bed mats first." She ignored her fears and remembered to move forward and pray.

The rain beat against the jungle canopy. Mary kept her ears alert for the snarl of a leopard and hoped the drenching rain would stop any wild animal.

With Annie on her hip, she set off over the muddy path. Her oldest boy carried the chop box, filled with bread, tea, and sugar. The younger boys followed with cooking pots, both of them wailing. Janie followed crying.

"Sing, Janie. We've got to make noise to keep the animals away."

After an hour of hiking, the children were weary and wet. Their pace slowed. "When will we be there?" Janie cried. "My feet are tired."

"Keep moving, children. I know you're sleepy. We'll be there soon."

Mary sang. Mary prayed. After a three-hour hike, they arrived in Ekenge in the middle of the night, soaked and weary.

The village was quiet. No fires, no noise, no sign of life. Had warriors come through and captured the people?

A few slaves and two young boys rustled out of a hut.

"Where is everyone?" Mary asked.

The slaves and boys shook their heads.

"I forgot," Mary said. "You speak Bantu and I speak Efik."

Using gestures and a few words that Mary could understand, the slave boys explained that they were guarding the village while everyone else had gone to a neighboring village for a funeral.

Mary hoped Chief Edem and the villagers wouldn't come back drunk. Drinking alcohol was customary in the villages, especially for large gatherings. Drinking meant vile tempers and fighting.

The boys led Mary to an old hut. Rain dribbled down the walls, dripped through the roof, and ran across the floor.

She directed the boys. "Set the boxes on the dry spot over there. And, Janie, you can rest on the box with Annie."

Mary untied the pots from the boys' necks and set one under the dripping roof to catch water. Then she pulled the wet clothes off each child, stuffed the clothes in the roof to block the drips, and huddled together with the children to keep them warm. "Mr. Bishop will be here soon with the dry clothes."

The Ekenge boys delivered an armful of twigs. Mary stacked them and lit a small flame. The children blew at the twigs until the flame began to grow. Mary set the pot of water over the fire then pulled off her boots and rubbed her aching feet. Even in the downpour outside, she heard a clamor and then a huffing Mr. Bishop ran in.

He bent at the waist to catch his breath. Water dripped from his hair and clothes. "I tried to run, but the trail was slippery."

"You look like you could use warm tea. Where are the boxes?"

"The paddlers wanted to sleep," Mr. Bishop said. "They'll bring the supplies in the morning."

Mary felt her neck heating. "The children need dry clothes and sleeping mats. Tomorrow is Sunday. We aren't unloading the trunks on the Lord's day of rest."

Exasperated, she scrambled through the box of clothes Mr. Bishop had carried and dressed the children for bed. "Those men are afraid, not sleepy."

She tried to tug on her boots, but they wouldn't slide over her swollen feet. She tossed the boots on the floor. "I'll go barefoot."

"But Miss Slessor, the trail will cut your feet."

"You mind the children, Mr. Bishop. I'll be back," she said, ignoring Mr. Bishop.

An Okoyong slave boy carried a lantern for Mary as she bolted down the path to the river. The tree branches slapped at her face, and the roots in the path cut her feet.

Mary found the canoe tied to a tree branch, resting ten feet away from the riverbank. Her dress billowed up to her armpits as she waded deeper and deeper, and jerked the tarp off the sleeping men. "Every one of you, get up now!"

"Okoyong!" The frightened paddlers jumped.

No longer sleeping, the men held their paddles like spears.

"Ma Slessor?"

"Can you help me, gentlemen? I need boxes brought to the hut tonight. Who's willing to follow me?"

A paddler extended his hand and helped Mary into the canoe. "We will go."

"Thank you. There's nothing to fear but this treacherous weather. The Okoyong are away at another village."

Two days later, the rain had stopped and the sun beat down on the village. Mary looked at the equipment the paddlers had carried from the river. Among all the boxes, baskets, and trunks sat a foldable organ, a door, and several windows for her future home. Her trunks wouldn't fit inside the tiny hut.

Mr. Bishop hung the door and a window in the hut before he left on Wednesday. "You've got a door now. I think you're protected from a wild animal coming in your hut. Do you need anything else, Miss Slessor?"

"Constant prayer. Thank you for your kindness, Mr. Bishop."

Mr. Bishop and the crew disappeared down the grassy knoll into the jungle.

Mary surveyed the village. Set in a clearing away from the jungle, the dirt paths were littered with bones. The village stunk with animal dung. Rows of human skulls lined the outside of the palaver hut, which looked more like a shrine to the dead than a meeting house.

For twelve years, she'd dreamed of working in the deep jungles of Africa. Living here would be the biggest risk she'd ever taken.

Later that week, the quiet village came to life as the natives returned home. Guards tramped in first, followed by a group carrying Chief Edem. He wore an elaborate red-and-white feathered headdress, a perfect spot for a bird to perch, Mary thought.

The men lowered Chief Edem to the ground, and he walked straight to his hut without even a nod. Surely he'd seen all her trunks outside the hut as he passed.

The village elders followed Edem. A band of hunters carried spears. Then came Chief Edem's wives and other free women. The slaves came last. The children darted in and out of the women's legs, playing tag and laughing. At the end of the procession, two men carried a dead carcass tied to a pole.

Blood oozed from the animal. Mary recognized the grayish-brown fur of a monkey. She watched the slaves erect a pole and then hoist the dead monkey over a fire to cook. The elders and other free men propped themselves against trees and snoozed.

Inside the hut, baby Annie cried. Mary stepped inside, but gasped. A native woman squatted on the floor of the hut holding the baby's hand with her finger.

Dressed in a yellow tunic and hat, with rows of beads around her neck, this large woman raised her finger to her lips and handed the baby to Mary. "Sh-sh-sh." The lady whispered in Efik. "I am Chief Edem's sister, Ma Eme Ete."

Mary cradled Annie in her arms while Eme talked.

"I used to live in an Efik-speaking village. I was the senior wife of the chief." Eme's eyelids dropped. "When my husband died, the wives were blamed. The slaves were ordered to dig a pit and the village elders were ready to throw us in.

"The witch doctor lined up the wives in a circle, cut the head off a chicken, and threw the headless chicken into the middle of the circle. He said the chicken would stop in front of the guilty one. It stopped between me and another wife. The witch doctor chose her, broke her arms and legs, and threw her into my husband's grave."

Mary shook her head.

"Now I live here in my brother's village. He owns a lot of land in this territory. His slaves live on farms away from this village. Chief Edem is a powerful man. I answer to him now that I am a widow."

Eme Ete stood. "He allows me to walk freely, but a free woman must have her husband's permission to speak to others. Edem does not know I am here. We must not be seen talking alone, or we will be killed."

"Eme, please come to worship services tonight."

"I'll bring Edem." Eme whispered. "Our friendship must be secret. I warn you—watch yourself."

14

The New Hut

Edem finally gave Mary a hut big enough to hold her supplies without moving them in and out each night. Right away, Mary threw herself into cleaning the new hut. In wandered the slave boy that had carried the lantern for Mary the night she arrived. He picked up a broom and began to sweep.

Mary had learned enough Bantu to have a conversation. "What's your name?"

"Ekpa," he answered and continued working.

The hut had no windows, so Mary knocked a hole in the wall. Ekpa knocked holes too, then gathered the sticks and mud that had fallen from their work. When Mary scrubbed walls, Ekpa scrubbed walls and patched holes. While they worked, Mary asked questions and pointed, and Ekpa taught her Bantu words. After a week, the hut was ready.

Mary decided she had to tell Ekpa about Jesus. She prayed that God would help him understand. "Jesus is the true God in heaven, not these clay idols the people worship. He's the one who created you. He loves you, Ekpa. God wants you to believe in Him. Come to worship services and school. I'll teach you how to pray and read the Bible."

The next day Mary began transferring the trunks to the new hut. Ekpa hadn't yet shown up. Mary made her way through the village with an armload of supplies and her children loaded with as much as they could carry. Further up from her hut, people gathered near the palaver hut. Neither Chief Edem nor Ma Eme had told her about a meeting.

A shrill laugh coming from the palaver hut chilled Mary's spine. She ran toward the hut. She found a pot boiling on the fire and assumed the people were meeting to eat, but why here? Why now?

She pushed her way through the crowd. In the middle of the meeting area, an elder stood fully decorated with feathers tied to his legs and arms, white paint streaked across his nose, forehead, and chest. Bangles of shells shook, as he paced. Mary couldn't understand what he was saying. Was this some kind of celebration?

Her view still blocked, she wiggled her way to the front. There on the other side of the hut, flanked by two men holding his arms, Ekpa stood with his hands chained together.

The scene flashed in front of Mary . . . boiling pot, chanting, palaver hut . . . suddenly, she understood. This was a boiling oil ceremony.

The elder made his way to the pot and scooped the boiling liquid.

"Stop," Mary yelled. She pushed her way toward Ekpa, but men blocked her while the other men dragged Ekpa forward.

Ekpa, unable to move his hands, tensed his body and held his head back.

"No!" Mary screamed as loud as she could as the elder poured the hot liquid on Ekpa's hands.

Ekpa fell to the ground, crying from the pain, as the boiling oil seared his skin.

"He's just a boy!" Mary stood nose to nose with the elder. He snorted at Mary like a bull ready to charge. She didn't care even if he burned her next. "Give me the ladle," she screamed, "and I'll try the oil on you. You heartless creature!"

The elder opened his mouth like an animal about to bite and then spit in Mary's face.

Never had Mary felt such rage. She stomped her foot and bared her teeth as if she were a wolf ready to tear him apart. "Carry Ekpa to my hut."

The jeering crowd hushed. The elder backed away from Mary and then directed the men to follow her directions.

Inside Mary's hut, Ekpa rolled back and forth on the floor, holding his wrists, and moaning. Tears trickled down his face.

"I'm sorry this happened, Ekpa. Let me give you some medicine," she said tenderly. "Dear Lord, I pray no infection will result from the damage to Ekpa's skin. Only You can heal this burned flesh."

Doing her best to comfort him, Mary stayed up with Ekpa all night, wiping his forehead, singing and praying while he groaned in pain.

Ma Eme came the next day.

Mary felt her stomach twist. "Was Ekpa punished because of me?"

"He didn't participate in a hunting party so he could help you. They punished him for deserting tribal customs."

Someone had almost died for helping her. Mary felt as if she'd been stabbed.

Over the next few weeks, Ekpa's burns healed. "You're ready to move to your mother's hut, Ekpa. But come to school every day."

Ekpa smiled and hugged Mary's waist.

The villagers saw that not only did Ekpa live, but he also went to Mary's hut to sweep the yard, gather firewood, or play games with the children. After that, long lines of sick men, women, and children came for the white woman's medicine.

Mary spent her mornings helping the sick and injured. She learned Bantu quickly and began teaching school to a hundred children and a few adults. After the school session ended each day, Ma Eme slipped in to visit and drink tea. More and more, the natives of Ekenge felt like family to Mary.

One morning from the window in her hut, Mary watched a stranger enter the village. He wore only earrings and a grass skirt. His face had no paint marks of a warrior, and he carried no spear. With his walking stick and sack, he walked directly to Chief Edem's hut. In a moment, guards surrounded the stranger, and a crowd gathered.

Mary made her way through the noisy commotion. The stranger waved his arms in the air while he talked, but as soon as Mary reached the stranger, he stopped talking to Chief Edem.

He turned to Mary. "The talking drums say you can cure sickness. Our chief is dying. We can pay you to save him." He opened the sack and set four brass rods and a bottle of alcohol on the ground.

Chief Edem sat on a wooden stool in the shade. Ma Eme sat next to Chief Edem. Servants stood beside the chief, waving away the flies and mosquitoes.

Mary's heart leapt. She had wanted an opportunity to go to another village, and here was an answer to her prayers. "I will come."

The man motioned. "Hurry. My village is a day's walk away near Cross River."

Chief Edem stood. "I do not give you permission."

Mary pleaded. "The medicines might prevent death—a chief's death."

Crossing his arms, Chief Edem said, "My protection only extends an hour's walk beyond our village."

She had to ignore her fears and Chief Edem's fears. "If this chief dies, his family will be murdered."

Chief Edem shook his head. "This is a trick. You cannot go."

"Chief, the messenger said they are already digging the grave for his wives and slaves."

"Edem," Eme tapped her brother's shoulder, "if the chief dies, their village might blame us and seek revenge."

"The rivers are swollen from the rain. You cannot cross them." The shells in Chief Edem's necklace rattled along with the excuses. "It is elephant country."

That night, Mary didn't sleep. Was this a trick to kill her? Should she go without Chief Edem's consent? She prayed. She wouldn't allow herself to worry any longer.

Before dawn, Mary made up her mind. She had to follow God, to go into the world and preach His gospel. She looked through the window at the silent village. Dogs rested next to the huts. The goats slept. Mary prayed, dressed, and waited for the rooster to awaken the village before she went to Chief Edem's hut.

"I've thought all night, Chief Edem," Mary said. "What if you were sick?"

Chief Edem paused for a moment. "If their chief dies, they will kill you."

"Chief, if a soul can be saved, it's worth any risk—even death. Have you forgotten about the white woman's God?"

Chief Edem uncrossed his arms and nodded. "I sent the messenger back."

"What?"

"He is to send back an escort of free women and armed men to protect you. If they arrive, you may go."

"But, Chief Edem . . . the journey will take a another day. The chief might die."

"Necessary!" He yelled and pounded his fist. Then his voice softened. "For your safety."

Mary didn't know if she should scream at the delay or hug him for his consent. She reached for his hand and squeezed. "God bless you, Chief Edem."

When her escorts arrived, Mary gathered her children. "Ma Eme will take care of you." She kissed them good-bye. With her medicine bag and Bible, she left Ekenge not knowing if she'd return.

15

Saving the Chief

Four armed men led the way, followed by the messenger and then Mary. The free women walked behind Mary with more armed men trailing at the end of the line. What was Chief Edem protecting her from? Cannibals in the jungle?

Her skirt swelled to her waist as they waded through an overflowing stream. On the slick and muddy path, fallen trees blocked the trail in some spots. The rain came down so hard Mary could hardly see. Mud stuck to her soaked clothes. A few paces ahead, the messenger stopped for Mary and those behind her to catch up.

"I wish I could move faster, but this skirt . . ." Mary held the hem that felt like a heavy sack. Mud stuck to the bottom. What was she doing wearing a long skirt in the jungle?

Mary looked at the free women walking with her. Some wore a cloth wrapped around their waist. The men marched in their grass skirts. She had to move faster.

Stepping behind a moss-covered tree, she unbuttoned her outfit, unlaced the boots, and laid them in a heap on the ground. Clumps of mud fell from her outfit. She worried the people would lose all respect for her, but the weight of the clothes slowed her down. Her arms and legs dangled out of her white petticoat, but compared to the natives, she was still overdressed.

A couple hours later the rain stopped and the group came into a clearing with grass as tall as Mary's shoulders. Her eyes followed the trampled grass where elephants must have traveled. The clouds parted and the sun peeked through as Mary entered the village. Besides the usual clapping to ward off animals, the group was solemn. *Jesus, protect me.*

They walked past men guarding a deep hole. A grave! Mary had seen one before but never this big. *Oh, Lord,* she prayed, *don't let the chief die.* The cavity looked big enough for elephants. Her stomach lurched knowing it was prepared for hundreds of people whose arms and legs would be broken before they were thrown into the pit alive and left to die.

Whenever a chief or high-ranking elder died, the custom was to throw the chief or elder's entire household, wives, slaves, and children into a pit. She had to convince the natives to value the lives of their families, but how? *Help me, Lord. I can't fight these heathen traditions, but You can.*

Carved statues, rows of beads, scattered shells, and piles of bones carpeted the ground in front of each hut. Forty or more guards, dressed in loincloths and armed with spears and guns, surrounded the chief's hut.

Soft muffled cries came from the women huddled on both sides of the hut. Children clung to their mother's legs. The guards stepped aside as Mary walked through a maze of spears.

Inside the chief's hut, gray smoke filled the room and stung Mary's eyes. There in the corner lay the sick chief. The back wall of his hut was lined with elephant tusks, snake skins, and skulls.

From the time she'd spent in African villages already, she knew the small skulls were probably monkeys, others possibly leopards, but some others . . . human? Would her head be among the collection? Or would she join his wives in the grave? *Even though I walk through the valley of the shadow of death, Thou art with me.*

The chief lay still, his stomach swollen to the size of a melon. Mary held his limp hand and then placed hers on his forehead. His skin felt fiery. "You have a fever, Chief."

"Father, I beg you," Mary rummaged through her bag for medicine and prayed in English. "Save the chief, his family, his village."

Mary gave the chief medicine. She knew the chief suffered from not only fever and infection, but also malnutrition. She hurried outside to find him a meal. "Bring soup. The chief needs food."

The women froze with fear. No one volunteered.

Angry, Mary could feel her neck tingling. "I didn't travel this far to watch a man starve to death." Her tone was harsh.

"If the chief dies," a young woman answered, "whoever prepares his food will be killed."

Mary tried to calm the urgency in her voice. "Who will trust in the Great Chief of heaven to protect you? Your human chief is too weak to live without food."

An old white-haired woman stepped forward. "I will."

The stars twinkled in the sky by the time Mary had spooned a few drops of yam soup into the chief's mouth.

The long trip had fatigued her, and Mary felt like she had a fever. But she stayed with the chief all night, listening to his labored breathing, reading the Bible out loud, and praying. The women and men waited quietly outside in the moonlight like a collection of mourners, preparing for their own funerals.

The next morning, Mary tilted the bottle. The medicine would be gone before the end of the day.

The chief's swelling had gone down, but he was still sick. Mary found the messenger who had led her here. "The chief needs more medicine right away. Ekenge is too far.

Ikorofiong is closer. Can you run to the missionaries there? They'll have what I need."

He shook his head. "Anyone from our village would be killed if we travel in Ikorofiong territory."

"Someone must go!"

"Sorry." The messenger shook his head. "Wait—there is a man from Calabar who lives nearby. He is the son of a Okoyong woman and could travel without fear into Ikorofiong."

"Find him."

Mary stayed by the chief's side caring for him. Later in the day, the medicine arrived along with tea, sugar, and a letter from the missionaries, Mr. and Mrs. Cruickshank.

Over the next few days, the chief regained his strength and his fever passed. Mary went out to the waiting crowd. "Your chief will live. He is sitting and talking. We must thank God." Mary raised her hands in the air and looked at the sky. "Great Chief, we praise You for your mercy."

The drums beat the news. Mary spent the next days conducting morning and evening worship services. The guards laid down their weapons. The natives listened reverently. Her heart loved the people here as much as her Ekenge family, but she knew she had to leave.

"Come back. Teach us book, and we will build school," the chief promised.

"I will try to send a teacher." Mary knew the need for more missionaries was greater than the number of missionaries available. She resolved to pray harder. There were so many more jungle villages like this one that needed to hear the story of Jesus.

"Promise you will be our mother, our Ma." Women cried and children clung to Mary.

Mary knew addressing someone with the title of mother was the greatest compliment an African could give any woman. The trip had been hard but worthwhile. She

was seeing her dream come true right before her eyes—
God at work in lives of those who had never heard about
Him before.

    " 'Tis an honor to be called your Mother."

16

Safe Territory

Mary's daily responsibilities grew in Ekenge—nursing, teaching, preaching, and, now that people trusted her, listening and resolving disputes. Each day ended with a worship service. One evening, Mary played the portable organ, donated from Duke Town, while the children drummed, shook their tambourines, and danced.

Above the music, she heard noises and immediately pushed her way through the crowd at the palaver hut. *Oh, God, please don't let this be another burning oil ceremony.* Before she could see anything, she heard desperate cries.

Reed torches lit the drummers' faces. The drumbeat throbbed in her ears. In the middle of the hut, a woman lay on the ground with her hands and feet tied to a stake.

Dancing around the woman, a warrior wearing a jaguar suit shrieked and yelled. A pot of oil bubbled on the fire. The warrior scooped a ladle of oil and turned toward the woman.

I have to stop this tragedy. Mary jumped between the warrior and the woman. The crowd stepped back, gasped, and ceased talking. The drummers stopped. Mary's heart beat wildly, like the day in Dundee when the bully swung the metal rope around her head. *God, help me.*

The warrior charged toward Mary. She held her position like a statue. She wouldn't run. She had to stand up to this beast.

She had to protect this woman even if it meant they poured the boiling oil over her. The natives believed that the oil would not hurt an innocent person. Mary held her body rigid and prayed the warrior wouldn't see her fear. She repeated Exodus 14:14 in her head. *The Lord shall fight for you, and ye shall hold your peace.*

The warrior stepped closer. Mary could smell the nutty odor of the hot palm oil. Fire licked the sides of pot. The oil was so hot that flames came out of it.

Face to face with Mary, he held his head back and let out a blood-curdling yell.

Mary didn't flinch.

All at once, he spun around, dropped the ladle to the ground, and disappeared through the crowd.

Mary knew the chief could stop the ceremony, so she rushed over to Chief Edem. "Save her life, Chief. One word from you and she lives."

The crowd hissed and hollered.

Chief Edem ignored Mary. He'd ignored her when she asked for a bigger hut and when she asked to help another village, but she needed his attention now. "Chief Edem!"

He still didn't answer.

Mary ran back, untied the woman, and pulled her up. "Go to my hut!" she yelled to the woman, running right behind her.

Safe inside Mary's hut, both women panted, trying to catch their breath. Mary wondered if Chief Edem would keep his word. Would her hut be safe?

Mary passed the water jar to the frightened woman. "Why did they condemn you?"

The woman shook her head as tears spilled down her cheek. "I paid a man a yam. He wouldn't leave until I gave him his wage."

Ma Eme slipped in for a visit.

"Death for giving someone a yam?" Mary couldn't fathom such a barbaric lifestyle.

"A married woman isn't allowed to give food to any man except her husband," Eme said. "The village is whispering about your God. Even Chief Edem wonders if God wants him to do kind things."

Mary's eyes filled with tears. "So Chief Edem's heart is finally softening."

"The people say you are the mother of us all—Eka Kpukpru Owo."

"I am God's ambassador to the Okoyong." Mary poured a cup of tea for Eme. "God is working. He saved the woman from death and me from death."

Mary closed her eyes and held her folded hands against her chest. *God, when will the Okoyong people change the cruel laws that rule their lives?*

For days, Mary heard nothing but the bleating of goats and cracks of twigs as people moved about the village. Even the children played quietly. Almost every day before the evening meal, Eme slipped in the back of Mary's hut. Ma Eme's information and advice had become invaluable to Mary.

"The people are stunned, Mary. No one confronts a chief or an elder and lives. But you have." Ma Eme leaned over the teapot to whisper. "There's talk that your God is more powerful than the chief."

"Of course, God is more powerful than man. He created man." Mary looked at Eme. "We are friends. What about you? You've seen the miracles. God saved me and others several times already. Don't you believe in Him?"

"I believe in Abasi." Eme fidgeted and looked away.

"Yes, you believe in an idol you call Abasi. What about the living God, the true Abasi? The only God. The God who created this beautiful jungle around us. The God who loves you. Won't you believe in Him, Eme?"

Eme stood. "We will talk another day."

Just as Mary finished teaching school one afternoon, one of Chief Edem's guards marched into her yard.

"Chief Edem needs you. Hurry. He is sick."

Mary ran alongside the guard, thinking of the consequences of a sick chief—blame. Someone would be blamed for his illness, someone innocent. *Lord, please help me help Chief Edem.*

As she stepped into Chief Edem's hut, the horrid smell took Mary's breath. She covered her nose in the crook of her arm. He lay on his stomach. Tears trickled down his cheeks. On his back was a bump the size of an orange. She'd never seen an abscess so big.

Mary boiled water, gathered herbs, and wrapped them in a moist warm cloth.

Chief Edem screamed when she placed the cloth on his back.

"I'm sorry, Chief. It will be painful until the infection is gone. Hopefully, the poultice will help."

"Who is to blame for this?"

"No one. We all get sick." *Father, please heal Chief Edem.*

For two days, Mary cared for Chief Edem, changing the poultice and praying for his healing. In spite of her efforts, Edem's back remained red, swollen, and painful.

Chief Edem hit his fist against his wooden cot. "Your medicine does not work. Bring the witch doctor."

He'd spoken the words Mary dreaded—witch doctor. "Chief Edem, healing takes time. Please, let me stay and pray with you."

"Go!"

Outside, people armed with swords and guns drank and quarreled. Mary stood in the middle of the swarm, pacing and praying.

An hour later, the toothless witch doctor strutted up to Mary and dropped a dirty cloth at her feet. A collection of nails, eggshells, lead shot, and a pouch of gunpowder spilled on the ground. "Look what came out of Edem's back. What good is your God?"

Mary knew the witch doctor hadn't pulled those items from the Chief's back. He had brought the collection with him in a pouch.

"A woman is to blame." The witch doctor sneered. "We will find her and chain her up."

"How can a woman cause his sickness?"

"By casting a spell." He sounded like an animal growling when he spoke.

"Stop lying. Your superstitions are killing innocent women." Mary could feel her jaw tighten. She knew the witch doctor used trickery and lies to fool the natives into believing in witchcraft. If the witch doctor used the poison eseré bean, a practice called chop nut, the women would die.

The poison bean was ground into powder and mixed with water. The people believed that if you were guilty, you would die after drinking the mixture. If you were innocent, you would vomit. She'd challenge the witch doctor, Chief Edem, and their deathly customs if it saved a woman's life, no matter what happened to her.

"What is your proof?" Mary screamed in the witch doctor's face.

Nose-to-nose, the witch doctor hissed and snarled in her face. His breath smelled worse than the animal stench in the village. "I will shake the bones and find out."

He shook a bag of small bones on the ground. "The bones say the punishment is," he paused and pointed his bony finger. "Chop nut!" He began dancing and chanting. Women fled to their huts, screaming and crying.

Mary knew the women were running from the deadly bean, running to save their lives. Which woman would he choose?

The witch doctor gave orders to Chief Edem's guards. Within minutes, they dragged a group of women to Chief Edem's yard and chained them to the fence.

"Thirty women! Release them." Mary spoke firmly. "These women couldn't hurt the chief."

The witch doctor pounded the poison eseré beans with a rock and scooped the powder into a coconut cup.

Mary stood guard by the women.

He pointed. "These women practice witchcraft against our chief. Tomorrow they will drink the cup." He cackled. "The guilty will die."

"Speak the truth, you coward. One swallow of an eseré bean kills anyone." Mary was angry and ready to fight. She wanted to reveal the truth, but the natives believed anything the witch doctor said. "The people believe you. Don't you realize how you deceive this village? Why don't you drink the poison?"

The chained women sobbed and begged for help. "Ma, save us." Children stood on the edges of the yard reaching and crying for their mothers.

Mary held the women's hands and wiped their tears like a mother checking on a hurt child. "I am praying for your freedom."

One woman shook her head. "How . . . do . . . you . . . pray?"

Mary knelt next to her. "Just talk to God like this. 'Father in heaven, I ask you to protect my life and the lives of every chained woman. Please change Chief Edem's mind and stop the witch doctor.'"

The woman repeated Mary's words.

Late into the night, Mary continued praying with each woman. "God gave us all the chance for eternal life. If you believe His promise, you'll live forever in heaven. Pray. Believe Him."

The women were parched from the heat. Mary slipped each a sip of water when the guards weren't looking. She waited all night, hoping the guards would fall asleep so she could sneak them food, but the guards stayed awake.

17

Chief Edem

In the middle of the night, Chief Edem called for more medicine from the witch doctor.

"I removed more from Chief Edem's back." The witch doctor held up feathers and rib bones. "Round up more women," he cried.

Guards stormed into huts and shackled more women to the fence.

When the rooster crowed, Mary couldn't stand another minute. She stomped into Edem's hut. "Chief Edem, order your guards to release the women."

Chief Edem balled up his fist and banged it against his cot. "How dare you order me? I am being tortured by the gods for allowing you into this village."

"You have an infection. You are not being punished."

"Guards." Chief Edem yelled. The men rushed into his hut. "I do not want to be near this God-woman. She brings trouble to my village. Move me to my farm."

Mary knew Chief Edem had a hut on his land not far from the village where his slaves tended vegetable crops.

Chief Edem turned his head toward Mary, his jaw clenched. "Do not follow me or I will burn your hut."

She felt hopeless as she watched the guards carry Edem and drag the chained women away. An eerie silence fell over the village.

Prayer was her only resource. Mary stayed on her knees. Another day passed, and the guards whisked away more women to the farm. The mood in the village was quiet. No one knew what to expect with their chief sick. Even the sky stayed overcast and gray.

Two days later Ma Eme came to talk with Mary. "Edem is getting better," she whispered.

Mary held her hands against her chest and looked up. "Oh, thank you, God!"

Ma Eme's face turned grave. "But he's already condemned the women to death. If he goes back on his word, he'll be a coward in the people's eyes."

"We must convince him to save the women." Mary could feel her heart beating fast. She felt hopeful. If Edem changed his mind and saved the women's lives, this would be a first for their village.

"Go tell your brother the people will respect him for saving the women. Tell him he will show more bravery by keeping the women alive."

"Ah, you are very clever." Ma Eme smiled. "My brother will show great courage if he accepts this idea." She paused and touched Mary's arm. "I remember how scared I was when my husband died. You are good for our village."

Now would Chief Edem defy the customs or would the women die?

The sun broke through the clouds, revealing a brilliant blue streak of sky. Chatter and laughter floated through the air for the first time in days. Mary followed the sound to the ravine near the edge of the village.

A triumphant smile covered Ma Eme's face as she led the women back to the village—Chief Edem had released the prisoners!

When they saw Mary, the women surrounded her, patting her face, rubbing her arms and hair. "Sosano. Thank you."

Mary felt like she would burst with relief. "God saved you, not me. Thank Him."

Happy tears trickled down Mary's face as she lay in her bed that night thinking of how children ran to hug their mothers. *Sosano, thank You, God.*

Mary hadn't slept through an entire night since moving to Ekenge. Her hut was so close to Chief Edem's she could hear everything around his hut— drumming, dancing, and drinking. The fight with the witch doctor left her feeling drained like a dry stream bed. Exhausted, Mary rested in her hut, reading, writing letters, and studying her Bible.

A few days later, Mary woke to the sound of banging.

Chief Edem stood outside, and a guard motioned her over. "Building season is here." He grinned and led her to the chopping sounds in an outer area of the village, where men and women were clearing the land.

"A place of my own. Thank you." She'd finally have a private place to live. More than that, she understood Edem had finally accepted her as a member of the tribe.

Mary jumped in to help. Men cut tree limbs with axes, women dug roots with sharp sticks, and children carried away small twigs. Then, they dug trenches for four huts—one for her, separate huts for the boys and girls, and a kitchen hut.

Men stood on each other's shoulders and positioned tall forked branches in each corner for the roof. Mary and the women gathered smaller branches to rest in the forks. After the roof frame was built, they covered it with dried grass and more branches.

With everyone helping, the work continued over the next few days. Women carried jugs of water from the river to pour into a mud pit. They took turns stomping the mud and rolling it into balls, and then they spread it on the outer walls. By the end of the day, Mary was covered in mud.

Chief Edem directed two slaves to build a fire inside the huts. "They will watch the fires all night. The heat will kill insects and dry out the sap. In the morning, the women will plaster the inside walls for you." Edem nodded his head and smiled.

Work on the inside of the hut began next. The women showed Mary how to form a fireplace, counter, couch, and table with clay. One lady hollowed out an indentation. "Look, Ma. A place for your teacups." Then they stained the clay with vegetable dye and polished it.

Last, they wove mats for the roof. As soon as Mary moved in, she spent the first night writing a report to the *Missionary Record*.

> This year marks the beginning of thirteen years in Africa. I am hoping for a carpenter to put the doors and windows in my new hut since the Ekenge do not know how to do this work. Wild animals could come through the holes for the doors and windows . . .

One summer evening several months later, Mary had just finished evening worship with her children. She made sure each child memorized scripture and learned the Scottish hymns she had learned as a child. She served her favorite meal of fresh corn stew. The children giggled as a couple of scraggly chickens pecked at the food they dropped.

She turned toward the woods, thinking she had heard whistling and singing. "Children, I think I heard a Scottish hymn." She cupped her ear. "I do!" It had been over a year since she'd had a European visitor. She jumped up to straighten her skirt.

Suddenly there was yelling, as a short, thick-bearded man stepped into her yard, surrounded by several Ekenge men. Guns pointed at his head.

"Stop. Put down your guns!" Mary said. "He's my visitor."

The man bowed. "I'm Charles Ovens at your service, Miss Slessor."

"What brings you to Ekenge, Mr. Ovens?"

"Your letter, Miss Slessor. I traveled from Scotland to hang your doors and windows."

"You came all the way to Africa to help me?" Mary couldn't believe her ears or her eyes. Mr. Ovens handed Mary a bundled stack of letters and newspapers. "The latest news from Dundee."

"How I cling to the words from overseas." She turned to seven-year-old Janie. "Janie, get some stew for Mr. Ovens."

Mary read the letters from Scotland aloud to the children while Mr. Ovens ate. Then Mary led evening prayers. The children went to bed and the stars twinkled overhead while Mary and Charles Ovens talked late into the night. "There are thousands of people in the three villages here, but I get lonely for home once in a while. How long will you be visiting?"

Mr. Ovens smiled. "Sounds like your dream is to have a house big enough for all the children you've adopted. I'll stay long enough to build you a house, not a hut."

Mary placed her hand across her chest. "It's July, but it feels like Christmas."

One morning, Mr. Ovens left to work on the mission house, and Mary settled on a bench shaded by a large mahogany tree. Her children and ten native boys sat cross-legged, practicing their alphabet on slates.

"What's that?" A boy dropped his stick. Several others jumped up, looking toward the forest.

A chill ran down Mary's spine. She'd never heard such a scream. Setting down her Bible, she stood, wiped her hands on her apron, and tried to look calm.

What did the scream mean? Was someone bitten by a poisonous snake? Or attacked by a leopard? It didn't sound like an animal. If the noise had been a war cry, the shrill yells would not have stopped. But this wasn't the sound of a war party. One scream, then silence—that was the sound of fear . . . or of death.

18

Etim

Summer 1889

Mary cocked her head to listen again but heard only the wind swishing through the trees.

"School's over for the day, children." Mary's heart felt ready to leap from her chest. A sound like that meant trouble. *Prepare me, Lord, with Your wisdom, strength, and protection.*

Mr. Ovens' assistant, a native man from the Calabar Mission, sprang from the woods. "Miss Slessor! Miss Slessor! Mr. Ovens said to come quickly. There's been an accident."

Mary ran for her medicine bag and sprinted through the woods behind the messenger.

In a small clearing not far from the land Chief Edem had given for the mission house, Mary could see a man pinned underneath a fallen tree. Mr. Ovens held the end of the tree, frantically trying to lift it.

"It's too heavy to lift alone," he said, panting and sweating. "No one will help, Mary."

Mary bent to check on the trapped man and gasped. "It is Etim. The chief's son." She barked orders to the crew of workers watching. "Help lift the tree."

The men shook their heads. "Sorcery."

Mary clenched her fists. "Help him! You will not die, but Etim *will* if you don't help."

She turned to Charles. "They're afraid to touch him for fear they'll be blamed for the accident. Accidents aren't accidents in the bush. They believe in witchcraft. Since he is the son of a high chief, people's lives are in danger already."

Again, Mary ordered the men to help. And this time, in spite of their mumblings, the native men followed Ovens to the side of the tree.

Mr. Ovens called, "Lift," and Mary interpreted. The natives heaved and dropped the huge tree on the ground next to Etim's cut and broken body.

Charles gathered tree limbs and then ripped off his shirt, tearing it into strips to tie the branches together as a stretcher. He and a worker carried Etim, while Mary led the way to Etim's mother, who was Chief Edem's head wife. The young man was conscious but barely breathing.

"Can you move your legs, Etim?" Mary worked fast, spooning pain medicine into his mouth and wiping the sweat off his forehead.

Etim moaned. He rolled his head from side to side, whispered a weak, "No," then closed his eyes.

Mary touched the side of his neck. "I feel a pulse. He's still alive. Just unconscious."

Etim's mother wailed.

Mary whispered to Charles. "We have to work quickly. The chief will call on the witch doctor to sniff out the guilty party for this accident. If Etim dies, he'll demand the lives of many more. Hundreds could die."

As Mary explained the situation to Charles, Chief Edem led the abia ibiong or witch doctor into the hut.

"The witch doctor will find out who is responsible for this." Chief Edem crossed his arms.

She felt her anger rise. The witch doctor would create more problems for this critical situation. "Leave him alone. He's injured, not dead."

The witch doctor glared at Mary, while he danced and hummed around Etim's unconscious body. In a gravelly voice, he announced, "Chief Akpo's village cast a spell on our village and caused this trouble."

Mary turned to Charles and whispered. "Find Ma Eme."

The witch doctor propped Etim's mouth open with a twig, lit a palm leaf, and blew smoke down Etim's throat and into his nose. Villagers hovered around Etim, yelling, trying to bring his spirit back to life.

Mary had to intervene. Many people in the village believed in God now. Others were beginning to question the practices of the witch doctor. She'd even seen progress with Chief Edem's attitude, but if he allowed the witch doctor to control this situation, the natives would follow his lead and return to their heathen practices.

"Please, Chief Edem. Don't turn to your old superstitions. Let me care for Etim." She began pulling bandages out of her medicine bag.

Edem crossed his arms and turned his back to Mary.

Mary ran outside. "Bring water," she yelled. Charles was leading Eme through the huge crowd outside the hut.

"Thank goodness you're here." Mary leaned into Eme's ear and whispered. Then Mary took the gourd of water handed to her by a native and slipped back into the hut. She rubbed water over the wounds on Etim's legs.

The witch doctor proceeded to work on Etim's body. Opening a sack, he rubbed hot peppers in Etim's eyes, and yelled in his ears, trying to call Etim's spirit back.

"Stop him, Chief Edem. He's hurting your son, not helping him."

Chief Edem stared at Etim, but avoided looking at Mary.

"Move out of my way, you evil man," she yelled at the witch doctor. "You're making Etim worse."

"Etim . . . my son—" Edem's gruff voice cracked.

Mary prayed continually. For two weeks Etim struggled between consciousness and unconsciousness. *God, I've tried everything. Help me, Lord.*

Whenever Etim woke, Mary worked fast. "Here, Etim, take a spoonful of soup." He turned his head.

"Medicine, Etim. Swallow." Etim would barely wake before he passed out again. Outside the hut, Mary could hear the uproar as the crowds grew. Word had traveled through the bush. Drunken chiefs and warriors arrived from other villages, ready for funeral celebrations.

Hoping to keep Etim's spirit alive, people flowed past, dropping charms of bones, feathers, and beads around his feet. "Spirit, don't leave Etim's body," family members begged. Some carried fruits and water jars. Everyone brought their tears.

Etim's chest scarcely moved. Mary held her ear close to his cracked lips, listening for his breath.

The witch doctor was still working on Etim when Mary realized his body had stiffened. She slipped out, quickly wrote a letter, and found one of Ma Eme's servants. "Rush to Duke Town with this letter."

When the witch doctor announced Etim's death, the village erupted like a volcano. People ran back and forth in every direction. The children copied their parents, darting among the chaos.

Mary hated to see what the children were learning from their parents. *God, if You were in their lives, this scene would be so different.*

She watched the witch doctor's every move as he began his rituals. He first slid skull bones around in the dirt with his finger. Then he smoked a pipe, watched the smoke curl, and he gave a war hoop. "The Kuri people's spirit came in the night and attacked Etim's spirit! Kill the Kuri!"

Edem stiffened his shoulders and raised his fist in the air. "We will avenge my son!"

Mary paced among the frenzied crowd and prayed. *Please, God, let Edem's warriors bring the Kuri people back to our village alive.* She knew there might be a chance to save them, if they didn't slaughter the entire village right away.

The high pitched war cries began. "*Iyyiyiyiyiyiiiii, iyyiyiyiyiyiiiii, iyyiyiyiyiyiiiii, whoop, whoop, whoop!*" Women set gourds of paint in front of the warriors. They covered their faces with stripes of white, black, and red. The men waved their spears, lit palm torches from the cooking fire, and danced around in a frenzy. The women stood on the outskirts swaying and chanting.

Chief Edem tied a band of ebony-colored feathers around his head and raised his arm in the air. "To Chief Akpo's village! Capture the evildoers!"

19

The Funeral

The war party marched away, and Mary prepared Etim's body for a funeral. If she could teach the natives anything, she'd show them how to honor a body in death, instead of throwing it into a pit. From a box of clothes donated to the mission, she selected suit pants and a jacket to dress Etim to look like a chief. Around his chest, she draped a rainbow of silk cloths—bright green, red, yellow, blues and purples. Then she painted his face yellow, slid rings on his fingers, wrapped a turban around his head, and topped the turban with a black and red feathered hat.

Mary and Mr. Ovens moved Etim outside and called a servant to help. "I need the chief's chair to set Etim in before he stiffens."

They propped the young man upright. In his right hand, Mary placed a silver-handled whip, a stick in his left, and slid an umbrella behind him. She knew the people believed in spirits, so she placed a mirror in front so his spirit could see how impressive he looked. "Doesn't he look like a regal chief? The spirit sees what has been done and is pleased," Mary said. She didn't believe in spirits, but she respected customs that didn't harm anyone.

"The people aren't used to a proper funeral. They need time to honor Etim," she told Mr. Ovens.

Two dozen women sang Etim's spirit on to the other world.

As Mary expected, the drunken and armed villagers paraded past and gawked. The scene delighted them, and they danced and called for more palm wine and liquor.

Soon, Edem and the warriors arrived back from Kuri, dragging two women, three children, and seven young men. More than fifty guards, with their loaded guns and swords, stood by the prisoners. Edem stomped to his hut, "The Kuri village was empty except for them."

Mary thanked God for Ma Eme's help and asked Him for help with the prisoners as the men shackled them to Edem's fence. *Lord, I see the terror in their eyes. Help me find a way to save the Kuri people.*

"Please don't cut off our heads! Make us slaves instead," the Kuri prisoners cried.

One of the warriors flashed a yellow-toothed grin at Mary. He pointed to the prisoners. "They are the murderers. And they need to suffer in this life before they suffer forever in the afterlife." He smacked the whip against the back of a male prisoner.

Mary jumped in front of the warrior to distract him. "Look at Etim!"

The warrior slackened the whip and stared at Etim's body.

Mary turned to Mr. Ovens, "If these people are murdered, my work in Ekenge is undone. We might be able to save the prisoners, but we have to keep a constant watch over them to make sure the warriors don't kill them. "I'll watch by night," Mary said, "and you watch by day."

The villagers turned into a mob of angry drunks after drinking alcohol for days. Tempers flared. They danced, sang tribal songs, and slashed their swords through the air as the intense heat magnified the stench of Etim's decaying body. The prisoners, lips blistered from the sun, quietly leaned against each other, too scared and too weak to beg for their lives.

Mary didn't sleep. She pleaded with Edem and the elders to save the prisoners.

"You want the prisoners?" an elder snarled. "Then make the dead live." He dismissed her with a wave of his hand. "Your God won't let the innocent die."

When Mr. Ovens wasn't guarding the guards, he built a coffin for Etim. As soon as the guards turned their backs or fell asleep, Mary and Charles slipped water to the starving and thirsty prisoners.

Days passed. Mary saw the witch doctor huddled with his warriors as she hid behind a bush to listen.

The witch doctor opened his clasped hand. "Poison beans. I have three handfuls in my pouch." He ground the eseré beans into a powder.

Now Mary was alarmed. She could see the witch doctor had more than enough poison to kill every prisoner. How could she stop the poison bean trial?

That night, two warriors unshackled one of the mothers and dragged her to Chief Edem's hut. Through a window slit, Mary watched the witch doctor mixing water in the cup. "Drink, you demon." He held the cup to the woman's lips. The prisoner clamped her lips together tightly. Mary ran inside, grabbed the woman's hand and pulled her out. "Run!" She pointed in the direction of the mission.

The startled witch doctor dropped the cup and poison puddled on the ground. Mary raced behind the woman. "Hurry before the warriors catch us."

Mary didn't turn back to see if anyone followed.

"Hide her, Mr. Ovens. She'll be safe here—if Edem honors his promise." Mary slammed the door. Would Chief Edem come on the mission property and take the prisoner back or kill her? He had promised the mission was a safe haven. Her feet pounded over the dirt path, her thoughts racing—she had to reach the other prisoners before another one was forced to drink the poison. *Don't let me be too late, Lord.*

Chief Edem stood in front of the prisoners, scowling at Mary. "You dare to interfere with our customs."

She answered Edem calmly. "You are not obeying God's law that is greater than your customs."

Mary stood by the prisoners for two more days, yelling at anyone who tried to come near. The Duke Town missionaries that Mary had sent for finally arrived. They set up a table, hung a white sheet between the palm trees, and lit a lantern.

A crowd gathered around. "The missionaries have come to honor Etim," Mary announced to the village. The lantern show was for entertainment. But Mary knew another missionary had used the lantern show to calm tempers down and hoped it would distract the people.

The missionaries held plates in front of the lantern and shapes appeared on the sheet. Mary explained each picture—a carriage, steam train, castle—but no one knew what she was talking about.

The crowd oohed. "White man's magic." Impressed, Edem finally released all the prisoners but one.

Mary ached for the one woman left as a sacrifice for Etim's death, but in the middle of the night the woman crawled into Mary's hut with her leg irons still fastened.

"Did Edem release you?"

"No," the woman whispered, "someone cut my chain— I don't know who saved me."

Mary suspected Ma Eme had helped. "I'll hide you here until it's safe and then you must run into the bush."

At Etim's funeral, the village threw a cow into his grave, instead of a human.

Two months passed before the Okoyong tribe settled and their drinking and fighting stopped. Mary looked to the sky and thanked God for preventing the bloodshed of the Kuri people. Never before had the Ekenge tribe had a funeral without sacrificing lives.

20

Romance

1890

Mr. Ovens built Mary a wood house, a medical office, and a church. To celebrate, Mary gave tours of the new buildings. The men in the village backed away when she led them to the staircase of her two-story home because they'd never seen stairs. The women giggled when they looked at themselves in her mirror.

Charles Ovens bowed in front of Mary. "My service here is complete. I'll be returning to Duke Town."

"Thank you, Mr. Ovens." Mary felt sad at the thought of Mr. Ovens leaving. She set her feelings aside. She had a new dream for the Okoyong village. The people needed work to occupy their time. The men drank rum or gin they had bought from other villages. Even the women drank. And when there was a party, she'd seen them giving the alcohol to the children for amusement.

She arranged for Chief Edem and his men to visit King Eyo and start trading. "Chief Edem, I am going to arrange a trip for you and the elders to trade with the Creek Town village."

Chief Edem stiffened his head and shoulders. "We are traders. We trade heads."

Mary knew Chief Edem's comment was only masking his fear. Creek Town and Okoyong were enemies. She convinced Chief Edem that Creek Town wouldn't attack them.

The trip to Creek Town was successful. King Eyo promised peace between the two groups and provided large canoes for the Okoyong to use to bring their palm oil and vegetables to trade with Creek Town.

Mary had been in Okoyong for two years when malaria symptoms began to slow her down. It was time to visit Duke Town for rest and treatment. On this visit Mary met Mr. Charles Morrison, a new missionary at Duke Town, who trained Africans to be teachers.

Over the next year, Mary spent more and more time in Duke Town with malaria episodes. She also spent time with Mr. Morrison whenever she visited. On the verandah in the evenings, Charles Morrison and Mary read books, discussed poetry, and studied the Bible together.

When she returned to Ekenge, they exchanged letters. Charles Morrison was becoming a dear friend. He was a scholar. He was a devout Christian. And she liked that very much. Or did she love him?

One night after returning to Ekenge, Mary lay in bed thinking she might be caring too much for Charles. Perhaps she should not visit with him so often. However, the following morning, she woke with a raging fever. Not well enough to travel, Mary wrote a note to let Charles know not to expect her to visit anytime soon, and Janie found a runner to deliver the letter to Duke Town.

The next day Charles Morrison arrived. "I'm taking care of you until you're better, my dear lady." For the next several days, when Mary wasn't sleeping, Charles fed her soup and read her favorite Bible passages from Psalms until her strength improved enough to travel to Duke Town.

Mr. Morrison and an Okoyong man carried Mary in a hammock to the canoe. Knowing the only way to completely recuperate would be a furlough to Scotland, Mary arranged for the care of her children before she left for Duke Town.

Charles clasped Mary's hand between his. "Mary, before you leave . . ."

"Yes?"

"God's painted you in my heart like a sunset. I can't let you leave without saying . . ."

"Yes?"

"When you return, will you marry me?"

Mary wished she could sit up and hug Charles. She'd promised God long ago she would do His will. Was marrying Charles Morrison His will? She was forty-two years old. Was she too old to marry?

Mary and Charles held hands and prayed, committing their relationship to the Lord. "God, will You guide our decision?"

"Our relationship cannot come before my commitment to God. Would you work with me among the Okoyong?"

"Certainly," Charles said. "We will be a missionary couple."

Mary smiled. "Yes, Charles, I will marry you, but we'll have to keep our engagement a secret until we notify the board."

He placed a ring in Mary's hand. "Wear it after you reach Scotland." For the next few days they discussed their plans until the ship arrived to take Mary back to Scotland. They would both contact the board for approval and pray. If the board approved, they would marry in Duke Town when she returned.

Several months later, after Mary had recovered from malaria, she wrote to the mission board for permission to marry and move Charles Morrison to work in Ekenge. She explained how the Okoyong needed a school for men. "With tools and training, they would be excellent carpenters. Mr. Morrison can teach them," she wrote. "And, I can no longer run the mission alone."

Mary waited and prayed.

Finally, the answer from the mission board arrived. "The mission approves the marriage, but Mr. Morrison's position is too important to lose. You will have to move to Duke Town until someone equally qualified can replace Mr. Morrison."

Shaken by the news, she let the words sink in for a month. She was in Scotland recuperating. He was in Africa. They had agreed that God's work was first, and she couldn't stop working in Ekenge after all the progress. She had no choice but to write and end the engagement.

> Dear Charles,
>
> My heart aches as I write this letter. I am sure you have received notice from the board. You are a great scholar and needed in Duke Town to continue your teaching. The good news is the mission board approved the idea of a training school. Our relationship is in God's hands and I will accept what He sees best for His gospel to be spread in Okoyong.
>
> My heart is full of love,
> Mary

In 1892, after Mary's health had improved, she stood on the deck of the ship, looking toward the African horizon, wondering what changes to expect after a year away from Calabar. She knew she wouldn't be seeing Charles Morrison in Duke Town. He had written her when he became sick; he had left Africa.

The newspapers reported the British had assigned a new man as consul to the Niger Coast Protectorate to establish British law from Calabar to the Cross Rivers. The British had never tried to bring law beyond the coastal villages.

A gig transported Mary to the Calabar shore. A man dressed in uniform extended his hand for Mary as she stepped out. Usually someone from the mission house greeted her. Why an officer?

"Please allow me to introduce myself. I'm Sir Claude Macdonald, the new consul. Will you join me for tea? I'd like to discuss some important matters with you."

Mary nodded as the consul extended his arm to her. "I've read the newspapers about the England's plan to enforce law in Africa. How are you going to govern the inland territories?"

"That's why I wanted to talk to you. Whenever I searched for help, everyone said I needed Mary Slessor. I threatened to take a ship to Scotland and bring you back."

"The doctors made me rest longer than I wanted— I was ready to swim back. Africa is my home." Mary smiled.

"Miss Slessor, I'd like you to be the new British vice consul."

Mary nearly choked on her tea, shaking her head no. "I want to get back to my people. There's so much work to do. We need scores of missionaries to reach the thousands of villages in Africa."

"You know the language. You know the people. You're the perfect choice, Miss Slessor, for the Okoyong territory. If you refuse to be consul, my only choice is to bring in an officer from England."

Mary considered the consequences of a new British officer, fresh from school trying to impose British law on the inland tribes. It would be a disaster. "I'd like to stop twin-birth killings and their cruel treatment of women," said Mary.

"Your word would be law, Miss Slessor," Macdonald said.

"The tribes would kill a new officer. They have to have someone who understands their customs and the language." Mary paused for a moment. "If it's what is best for the people, I will serve."

"I knew you would consent." Consul Macdonald smiled and handed Mary her official tools—a wax seal, a judge's robe, and slippers to wear as vice consul for the Okoyong territory.

21

The Vice Consul

1892

The happy crowd danced and cheered as forty-three-year-old Mary looked out from the deck of the boat. She arrived in Okoyong on a new steamer the church in Scotland had bought for the mission. After Mary's fifteen month furlough, she was met by the natives who lined the shoreline to welcome her home.

"A smoking canoe!" They pointed to the steamboat. "Our Ma is home."

Men carried Mary's boxes to her house. The children in the village gathered around Mary's yard, eagerly waiting for her to unpack the trunks. The church in Scotland always sent clothes, books, pictures, and trinkets for Mary to give to the children.

"We were afraid you would never come back," Ma Eme said as she helped Mary unpack. "What's this?"

"Red wax to seal official documents. I'm now the vice consul." Mary laughed.

Ma Eme raised her eyebrows. "Oo-oo. You have more power than a chief! If I hear about trouble, I will send a servant with a medicine bottle and ask for you to fill it. The bottle will be our secret code. Just follow the servant when he brings the bottle."

Mary smiled. "Thank you, Ma Eme. You have helped me since the day I moved here."

She could see progress. Ekenge people were giving their lives to Christ. Twin-birth deaths, human sacrifices, and raiding villages for slaves had nearly stopped. As vice consul, Mary spent her time resolving fights between chiefs in neighboring villages. When Ma Eme's medicine bottle showed up, Mary would tramp through the forest for a palaver between the fighting parties.

She wanted to teach people Jesus' way to solve problems instead of fighting. Under a kapok tree, Mary governed the palavers, wearing her robe and slippers. She taught the people how to state their problems and then listen to each other. She patiently knitted during the discussions that lasted hours, sometimes days. When Mary announced judgment, the chiefs had their own way of pledging agreement.

Mary hated the vow, called a *cut oath*, but she permitted some of the old ways. The chiefs cut each other's hands, rubbed salt, pepper, and corn into the cuts, and then chanted an oath to prove they agreed to the ruling. Then they licked each other's bleeding hand to finalize the agreement.

One night a runner arrived with Ma Eme's medicine bottle. Two villages, miles away, were on the warpath. Mary stamped her wax seal on a document for a runner to take ahead of her, hoping the official paper would delay any fighting before she arrived. Then she set off in the darkness alone, praying for God to shut the mouths of the animals.

In the darkness, Mary almost didn't see the huge cat standing in front of her, blocking the path. She had never carried a weapon when she traveled. Instead she prayed, knowing God heard her. She always hoped she wouldn't see a leopard. *Lord, please don't let me startle this leopard. Is this the end, Lord?*

The leopard growled and its bright eyes stared.

She stomped her foot. "Scat!"

The leopard stared at her and then sulked away into the bush. *Thank you, Lord!* Before daybreak, Mary arrived at the village. The guards swarmed around her with their spears pointed. The men's faces and chests were covered in paint, ready for war.

She prayed for God's help. "Salute," Mary said.

A warrior stepped forward. "What business do you have?"

"I've come to stop a needless war."

"A man from our village was beheaded. Blood for blood," the warrior said. "A woman has no power to stop this war," the warrior said.

"You have forgotten about the woman's God," Mary said.

An old warrior stepped through the line of guards. "Ma? Do you remember me? I was the sick chief you healed."

The old man was the chief that Edem had almost refused for her to help when she first moved to Ekenge. "I remember."

He knelt at Mary's feet. "Ma, we have started a war over one man's mistake. We will make peace instead of fight."

Many more times, villagers alerted Mary to trouble by calling, "Run, Ma, run." Mary always stopped whatever she was doing to help.

In 1896, Ma Eme suggested the village move to Akpap, where the land was better and the village would be closer to the traders. Mary arranged for two older Christian boys she had taught to stay in the villages in Ekenge and Ifako to teach school, and she planned to follow Eme to Akpap with her children. Mary had adopted a two-year-old girl named Alice. Janie was now fourteen, an excellent reader and Bible student. She and ten-year-old Annie helped Mary pack.

Chief Edem sat in his chair, smoking his long wooden pipe, watching men and women carrying loads on their heads, slaves leading animals, and children following. A slave held an umbrella over Edem's head to block the sun. People had been moving over the past couple weeks. Mary talked with Edem. "Eme is taking the entire village with her, Chief."

Patches of white hair had grown around Edem's temples. "Eme is right," he said. "The village needs to live closer to the river. The fields are dead."

"I have to go where the people need me." Mary swallowed hard. Chief Edem had changed, and she didn't want to leave him. "Are you coming to Akpap?"

Chief Edem crossed his arms. "My ancestors are buried here, and I will die here with them."

"Please, Edem, come. What will you eat?"

"Spear fish." He shrugged his shoulders and then took Mary's hands. His large hand covered both of hers. "Ma, you taught us to stop the old bush customs. The traditions had us bound, and you set us free."

In all the years she'd worked next to Edem, she rarely saw him express any emotion except anger. Mary felt both grief and joy. "God set you free, my dear friend."

Edem choked back tears.

"I'll come back." Tears streamed down her cheeks as she followed the trail toward Akpap.

Akpap was six miles from the Cross River and in more remote territory than Mary had ever lived. Almost everyone from Ekenge, except Chief Edem's household, moved to Akpap. Living on fertile land closer to the Cross River, farmers planted new fields. But the harmatten, or sandy dry winds, blew. Suddenly four babies died within a week. The harmatten only made people feel sick; it didn't kill people. Mary didn't understand the babies' deaths.

More people in the village began dying faster than Mary could bury them. Desperate to save as many people as possible, she sent a runner to Duke Town for help. The runner returned with a large white box of immunizations and a letter explaining the disease. She was fighting a smallpox epidemic.

Mary looked at the box of needles and worried it might be too late for Akpap. So many people had already developed the rash and fever. She raced to give immunizations to as many people as possible.

Mary worked day and night as the dead bodies piled up. She had no time or help to bury them. After seeing so many die, most villagers lined up for their shot, but one fierce-looking man cowered when Mary brought out the needle. He shook his head and refused. "No time to argue," Mary said. She punched him in the stomach and plunged the needle into his arm.

Even Ma Eme tried to avoid the injection. "I shouldn't have moved upriver to Akpap. Save your medicine. I am an old woman." Mary ignored her too.

When the vaccines ran out, Mary scraped pus on scabs from people who had been inoculated. With this she made more vaccines.

Finally, she rushed down the trail toward Ekenge. *God, help me reach Edem before the smallpox does.*

Old water pots lay toppled over, and vines covered empty huts. The village reminded Mary of her first night in Ekenge. No smoking fires, no men carving wood, no animals crawling about. Only an eerie silence and the smell of death. She passed decaying bodies.

Mary cupped her hands around her mouth. "Chief Edem."

No answer. She called for Edem until she found him inside his hut on his clay bed. A mass of bumps covered his arms, face, and chest. His eyes were swollen shut and red welts distorted his mouth.

Edem's hair and beard had turned completely white since she'd last seen him. "I am too late, my friend." Mary gave him water, but she knew the smallpox had infected him.

At midnight, Edem took his last breath. Exhausted from weeks of trying to save everyone and witnessing so much death, Mary curled on the ground beside Edem and wailed. She sat beside Chief Edem, singing hymns, allowing her tears to flow freely. "Chief Edem, you will have a proper Christian burial. I will not leave your body for the animals."

Dirt flew in the air as she dug inside the hut. A few hours later, Mary dragged Edem's body into his shallow grave. She hurried before the animals in the forest smelled the body and arrived for a feast.

"You won't need these weapons, but I will honor your traditions." Mary set Edem's gun, swords, and whip beside him. "If your tribe were here, they would build a shrine for you. But God has a home for you in heaven." Mary bit her lip and stifled a cry. "Did you give your life to the Great Chief, Edem?"

From two sticks, she formed a cross to top his grave. Weary, she trudged home to Akpap as the black night sky lightened into a deep purple then a rosy pink.

22

The Fight

1898–1902

After the smallpox epidemic, Mary collapsed. Charles Ovens arrived in Akpap to build a new house for Mary but found her in bed exhausted and grieving. She'd lost an adopted girl named Susan and Chief Edem. The board insisted Mary take a furlough, but she made sure her children had homes before she left. Annie returned to her parents, and Mary returned to Scotland with her girls, Janie, Mary, Alice, and Maggie. Their clothes were too ragged to travel in. At the Duke Town mission house, they found outfits which had been sent to the mission from the church in Scotland.

As soon as Mary had recuperated, the mission board arranged receptions for her. She encouraged the young people who were ready to serve Jesus to work in the mission fields where multitudes had never heard of Him. Mary shivered in the Scotland climate and longed to be home in Africa. After ten months in Scotland, Mary felt healthy and homesick and the mission approved her return.

Mary received a warm welcome home in Akpap. The drums beat the happy message, *Eka Kpakpru Owo*—the mother of us all has returned.

Charles Ovens greeted Mary. "I built a home worthy of the white queen of Africa. You were living in a donkey stall!"

News traveled quickly by way of the talking drums—over two hundred miles according to Ma Eme. Natives from other villages showed up regularly for advice and medical treatment. Mary's new home was also a nursery full of rescued babies. Mr. Ovens left to continue working where he was needed in the mission field.

Mary's dream of working with the Okoyong tribe had come true. She had served as a missionary for over twenty years. Now she wanted to explore new territory further inland and planned trips to explore the Cross River. Her goal was to learn about the Aros people in Arochuku, the old slave trading territory. From the river's edge, Mary walked miles into the forest, discovering villages tucked far away from slave hunters. Even deep in the jungle, the people had heard about "the white queen" and welcomed her.

Around the fires, the villagers told Mary what they knew. "The Aros are slave-traders and cannibals. They worship a god named Chukwu, and the priests are the only ones who see the shrine, the Long Juju."

Everyone had the same opinion—the Aros village was evil and scary, but the details of their lifestyle remained a mystery. In spite of what she learned, Mary still wanted to bring a gift to the people in Arochuku—the gift of salvation. "I want to talk to the priests and tell them about the real God."

"No, no, Ma, stay away. A white person has never entered their territory," the people in the villages said.

Mary didn't let anything discourage her. If God wanted her to talk to the Aros, He would provide a way for her to reach them. With some paddlers and her Bible, she continued her exploratory trips upriver, sleeping on a bed of leaves under the stars, getting closer and closer to Arochuku. She told everyone about the real chief, God. As the natives accepted Jesus, she left instructions for the new converts to build a mud-hut church.

Then Mary returned to Akpap. Janie, the eldest, managed the mission house and the younger children. She urged Mary to slow down. "You're fifty-two, Ma. Rest and let me do the work. I'm eighteen. I can take care of Mary, Alice, and Maggie."

"I may be slower from rheumatism, dearie, but I can't be idle." When her pain prevented her from working, she'd lie in bed, swing a hammock with her foot, and rock Dan, the new baby boy she had adopted.

The rainy season came. Overnight, the jungle paths swelled with growth. The smokes—the harmatten—followed. The wind blew fine sand that dried everyone's throats, noses, and impaired their vision, but didn't cool anything.

Mary had not had a visitor in almost three years. She continued her daily work in Akpap and weekend explorations on the river. During the late night hours, she wrote letters, studied her Bible, and prayed more than ever for God to help her reach the slave traders.

One morning a British officer arrived. Delighted, Mary hurried to greet him. "I'll put the kettle on for tea, and we'll talk. I'm starving for news."

The officer tipped his cap. "I'm sorry, Ma'am. I'm here to inform you the British government has ordered all missionaries to return to Duke Town."

"Ordered? Okoyong territory is peaceful."

"The Aros have blocked the river. British and African soldiers are assembling in Duke Town to attack the Aros. The situation is too dangerous for you to stay. Miss Slessor, a British steamer will transport you and your family to Duke Town tomorrow."

Mary didn't like being torn from her people. She had lived among the Okoyong in Ekenge and Akpap for fifteen years. The old customs had died away. The thought of war between the British and the natives saddened her. She had hoped to reach the Aros with God's message first.

In Duke Town gunboats crowded the harbor. A hundred and fifty British officers led thousands of African soldiers ready to fight the Aros. Mary learned from the British commander why they were going to fight the Aros.

"The Aros spread the word that their village had a powerful juju that could help them settle disputes and solve problems. This past December, eight hundred people traveled to Arochuku looking for the Long Juju. Instead, many of the people became victims of cannibals, except for a few who fled." Colonel Montanaro adjusted the collar on his uniform. "A hundred escaped to a British outpost. We've got to stop this terror and the only way is by force."

"Why were the missionaries removed?"

"The Aros hate British rule. We were concerned the Aros might hold missionaries hostage. You're better safe in Duke Town than a prisoner among cannibals."

In November, the gunboats left Duke Town and traveled until they reached the river barrier set up by the Aros. After months of preparation and weeks of travel, the battle began. The soldiers seized the river, then made their way through the dense forest, fighting the Aros. Hundreds on both sides died. The last few surviving Aros finally surrendered.

In March, 1902, after the battle, Colonel Montanaro personally escorted Mary back home to Akpap.

"As you know, Miss Slessor, the forest is a monster to navigate. No trails. Bushmen blocked any paths we found and fought us."

Mary nodded.

Montanaro continued. "On an island near the river gorge, we discovered a hut with a starving goat inside. It was the juju house. Large cooking pots and skulls covered the ground like seashells. As the group had told us, some of their people were blindfolded and taken across a stream to a cave. What we discovered was, instead of killing those who were blindfolded, the Aros sacrificed goats and poured the goat's blood into the river. The people on the other side watched the river turn red and believed people had been sacrificed to the juju god."

"They tricked the people who came for help," Mary said.

"There's more," Colonel Montanaro said. "The blindfolded prisoners were chained and sold as slaves to inland tribes. Those who didn't escape became the cannibals' meal. Long ago the Aros took the slaves to the coasts to sell to the ships bound for the West Indies or America. For decades, slave money has made them rich and powerful. That's why they barred the river."

Mary shook her head. "God can change their ways. I want to teach the gospel of Jesus to the people left in Aros."

"We dynamited the gorge. But the area is still dangerous. The other tribes are fighting for power since the Aros' defeat."

Back in Akpap, Mary planned her first trip as soon as she could. Now more than ever, Mary wished to talk with the Aros people. She didn't know how she'd reach their village in Arochuku, but she continued the exploratory trips up Enyong Creek getting closer each trip.

One Saturday, she gathered her son Dan and a crew of paddlers to row her up the Enyong Creek to visit a village. Canoe trips relaxed Mary, and she looked forward to a chance to curl up under the canopy with a book. Suddenly, the canoe began to rock, and everyone started screaming.

"Ma! Se Isantim. A hippo!"

A huge hippopotamus charged the canoe.

The paddlers tried to beat the hippo with their paddles. Mary checked on Dan to make sure he was safe. She prayed. Arms flailed. Water splashed. The canoe swayed.

The paddlers were skilled at staying clear of dangerous animals. Mary had never encountered a hippo up close before. Slapping oars at the hippo did no good. Mary yelled orders at the crew, but it did not help. The canoe was in pandemonium.

Mary grabbed a bamboo pole from one of the paddlers and smacked the hippo's nose. "Go away you beast!"

23

A New Chief

1903

As suddenly as it showed up, the gigantic animal dove under the water and disappeared. Mary stared at the water, praying the hippo wouldn't come back.

The men paddled the canoe to the middle of the river and continued on their journey.

"Ma, even the hippopotamus obeys you," the paddlers said.

"I thought we were going to get eaten!" Dan said.

"Dan, my son," Mary said. "Here's a lesson for you. Our country is full of danger. Never let a weakness overpower you."

When they reached the village, one of the paddlers brought Mary a chicken as a gift. "We would have drowned if it hadn't been for you, Ma," the paddler said.

"God's power protected us." Mary prayed with the paddler. After that, the man attended church and became a Christian.

In the spring of 1903, a new missionary named Janet Wright joined Mary in Akpap. On weekends, Mary explored the river villages alone while Miss Wright and Janie cared for the children.

Mary met the government boats on the Ikenutu beach at the Cross River. One weekend she walked the six miles to Ikenutu, but arrived too late and missed the steamer as it passed. The next weekend, she caught a boat. Colonel Montanaro helped Mary on board and talked as the boat glided over the Cross River.

"The tribes continue to fight each other for control of Arochuku. I'm on my way to negotiate a peace treaty." Colonel Montanaro shielded his eyes from a flash of sunlight breaking through the tree canopy. "You understand the natives and speak their language. Would you be willing to help?"

Mary smiled. *Thank You, God, for delaying my trip and putting me at the river at the right time.* "Yes, Colonel Montanaro, I will. Your invitation is an answer to my prayers."

Mary and Colonel Montanaro spent several days in Arochuku talking with the chiefs. She knitted under the shade of an umbrella while the chiefs discussed their needs.

"Miss Slessor, I cannot believe how patient you are," Colonel Montanaro said.

"Ah, that is lesson number one in Africa. No one hurries in this country. They pay attention to the rising and setting of the sun, not the minutes like we do."

The chiefs finally agreed on a peace treaty and began the cut-oath ceremony.

"I cannot look," Mary said as the chiefs cut each other's hands, "but I tolerate the natives' customs that don't cause deaths. Some of their traditions aren't worth fighting."

Colonel Montanaro congratulated her. "Miss Slessor, your skill with the tribes is astounding. You were able to satisfy each chief's concern and leave both tribes behaving peacefully."

"After working among the people for twenty-eight years, I know their way of thinking, but I credit God. He uses me to do His work."

Afterwards, the head chief bowed to Mary. "Make your home here. We will build you whatever you need."

Mary looked into the eyes of the chief, a man once called a savage. A man loved by God, even if he had lived a barbaric past. Her heart felt as if it would burst at the invitation, she was so full of joy at God's answered prayer. "As soon as I make arrangements at Akpap, I will be back." Mary hugged her Bible to her chest. *Oh, God, You made a way into the most impossible territory—the old slave headquarters.*

Fifty-six-year-old Mary left Janet Wright in charge of Akpap and resigned her position as vice consul. Over the past five years, little mud-hut churches had sprung up all along the river where she had explored and explained the gospel. She had given up her missionary's salary for six months to live on her own in Itu, an old slave-trading country closer to Arochuku.

The day finally dawned for Mary to leave Akpap. The river's edge seemed to be lined with everyone from Akpap, their cries as loud as thunder. The scene reminded Mary of the farewells in Creek Town and Ekenge, except instead of sloshing in the rain, there was a golden hue that tinted the sky. The early morning air was already scorching hot.

The new district commissioner, Charles Partridge, held Mary's arm as they walked to the canoe. It was hard for Mary to believe her children were growing up so fast. Twenty-two-year-old Janie had become a great help to her, teaching in the schools and taking care of the younger children. Annie was now a teenager, her namesake Mary was already eleven, and Alice was ten. When they all reached the canoe, Alice helped seven-year-old Maggie and four-year-old Dan aboard. Nine paddlers waited in the canoe while Mary said her goodbyes.

"I won't be close enough to send you the medicine bottle." Eme smiled, but Mary noticed a single tear trickle down Eme's cheek. "No one here wants you to leave. You've changed this village. Be careful. You're our White Queen."

"God changed the people, Eme. I'll only be traveling for a few months, dear sister."

Colonel Partridge saluted Mary. "You're the bravest person I've ever met. My officers wouldn't do what you're doing without their guns. I don't suppose I can talk you into carrying a weapon? A British doctor who lost his way in the forest was killed and—"

"Laddie, I know others have been killed, but I've never been attacked or wounded. The armor of God is all I need."

Colonel Partridge waved goodbye as the drummer began the beat for the paddlers. "I'll be checking on you in Itu."

Mary's crew traveled up the Cross River and then followed Enyong Creek west toward Itu. Vine-filled trees arched across the river. Orchids grew from fallen tree trunks. Overhead, silver-gray parrots squawked, and monkeys chattered. A blue kingfisher shot out of the water. The girls skimmed their hands along the water covered with thousands of water lilies.

Mary imagined this scenery was how the Garden of Eden must have looked. Unfortunately, she knew slave traders had hauled bound men, women, and children down this river to sell them as slaves. The thought of the slave trade angered her. She said a silent prayer to thank God that slavery was illegal and feasted her eyes on the "bonnie" paradise.

The rowers sang in rhythm as the paddles *swish-swashed*, *swish-swashed* through the water. They rowed past villages along the creek busy with women filling water pots and naked children splashing along the shallow edge. Mary dreamed of building schools and churches in every village.

They hadn't quite made it to Itu when a canoe shot out of a cove and headed directly toward Mary's canoe. Mary's heart thumped. Were slave traders still capturing people?

The canoes rocked as their bows bumped. A young native man stood and held his hand in the air. "Stop. I've been watching for you," the young stranger said as he handed Mary a letter.

"My master would like to talk with you."

Mary read the invitation. Without questioning the stranger, she told the paddlers, "Follow him." God would send her where He wanted.

A few minutes later, the two canoes scraped onto the muddy bank where a well-dressed man stood. He stepped forward. "Greetings. My name is Chief Onoyom Iya Nya. I have waited so long to talk to the God-woman."

Chief Onoyom led Mary to his home filled with European furnishings and seated her in a comfortable bamboo chair. "When I was a boy, a missionary came to this area. I led him into our secret village. Even though I was punished, I have never forgotten what he told the chief about God. I have been searching for God all my life."

"God has been seeking you too," Mary smiled at Onoyom.

"When I grew up, I became a chief and practiced the evil rituals. I traveled to Arochuku for the cannibal feasts. I grew rich. But then my house burned with my son inside. Is God angry with me?"

"I'm so sorry you lost your son. Children are so precious. Your tragedy was an accident, not God's anger. God has promised to be with us through our trials. He redeems us from our own destruction." Her heart filled with joy at Chief Onoyom's repentance. "The Bible tells us in Psalms, 'The Lord is merciful and gracious, slow to anger, and plenteous in mercy.' God says if you seek Him, you will find Him."

Chief Onoyom leaned forward. "I am so sorry for the way I lived. Can you tell me about the God I heard about as a boy? Is he your God?"

Mary smiled. "He is the true God who loves you and forgives you. His son's death on the cross paid for your sins. He asks that you believe in Him. Do you?"

"I believe."

Mary held Chief Onoyom's hand and repeated the Lord's prayer. Then she helped him confess his sins, ask forgiveness, and accept Jesus into his heart.

"You are God's child—a Christian. Follow God's leading no matter what." Mary continued reading the Bible to him.

His face beamed. "I want to build a house for God to share His story and praise Him for saving me from my ugly past."

"Chief Onoyom, follow your dream."

"I want God's house to be built with the best. Not a mud hut, but of wood from the juju tree." He furrowed his eyebrows. "But our people believe the juju tree is sacred. They believe bad comes to anyone who dares to cut the trees. The priests will probably kill me if I cut a juju."

"I have lived my entire adult life defying the African superstitions." Mary spent all afternoon talking with Onoyom.

"God made the juju tree. The heathen priests have no power over it. Before I leave, you need something." Mary handed Chief Onoyom the Bible. "You will find your Savior in this book. I will pray you will have a school and a teacher for your new church so you can learn to read this Bible. God is calling you. If God has placed this dream in your heart, He will help you build the church, even with the sacred juju wood."

"I am not afraid. I have eternal life now."

Mary stood and clasped Chief Onoyom's hands. "I dare you to ignore the superstitions and follow God."

24

The Cow

1905

On November 26, 1905, Chief Onoyom opened the doors of the new church. A few curious residents and visitors from villages all around Enyong Creek came for the first church service. But some town folk, who believed in spirits and predicted disaster for Onoyom, had fled when the carpenters felled the first juju tree.

The drums spread the news that the White Ma lived nearby, and Mary soon received requests from other villages. "We want to know God. Send a white ma like you to teach us book."

"Yes," Ma answered. She traveled along the road, teaching God's story and building churches everywhere.

The British built roads and bridges closer to inland territory. Mary worked tirelessly to reach the people before the British soldiers and traders did. She wanted the natives to understand God's plan for their lives. She knew if God's Word were planted first, the atmosphere would change, and their hearts would soften.

Back in Itu, Mary often received visitors—traders, missionaries, British officials, and soldiers. Colonel Partridge visited whenever he could. Mary grew very fond of all the "laddies."

"Mary Slessor!" Colonel Partridge waved. "I followed the churches along the river. They're cropping up everywhere."

Mary held a baby; another one sat by her feet wrapped in a brown paper blanket asleep in a milk-box cradle. "It's good to see you, laddie."

Colonel Partridge set a box down beside her. "Canned milk from the governor for the babies. Your reputation in Calabar and Britain spreads, Miss Slessor. Everyone wants to help the orphans."

The house swarmed with children, or her *bonnie bairns*, as Mary called them. Some of the children she raised until another Christian family adopted them. Some of the children she had raised had grown up and become Christian teachers at the churches she set up along the creek. Curious toddlers hung onto Janie's skirt, peeping at the officer.

"I've written the mission board asking for an orphanage and more missionaries. The babies are usually unfed and untouched. Not all survive, but every life is so *important*." Mary limped over to a milk crate to sit down.

"Miss Slessor, you can hardly walk."

"I'm small, lame, feeble. Ah, I'll tell you what they say in Scotland. I'm a wee, wee wifie, verra little buikit, but I keep going," Mary said in her Scottish tongue and picked up a baby from the milk crate.

"Mary Slessor, you need a rest, but I know you won't take one. I've brought something to help you stay off your feet." Colonel Partridge rolled a bicycle toward her. "You can at least stop hiking everywhere and travel by bike on the new roads."

Mary shook her head. "I'm fifty-seven years old, too old to ride a bike."

The children clapped and hovered around the bike. "Come on. Ride it, Ma."

Partridge winked at Mary. "Think how much faster you could reach the villages. I'll help you."

With Partridge's help, Mary climbed on the seat, balanced herself and then pedaled down the road. It surprised her, but she had no trouble riding at all. "I've got a good grip," she called to Partridge as he ran beside her. Mary sped faster and took off ahead.

The natives gawked and yelled, "Enan ukwah. Iron cow!"

Later that afternoon, Janie served tea, jam, and biscuits to Colonel Partridge and Mary.

"I'd like you to take up your former position as judge, Miss Slessor. You would be vice president of the native court. We need a clever person to enforce justice."

"If it will help my people and serve the cause of God, I'll do it."

Mary held court in a thatched building in Ikotobong. Wearing her court attire, she sat at a small round table to judge cases brought from natives throughout the region. Everyone preferred Ma's court over other British officials because she spoke their language.

Mary tried cases for stealing, murder, eseré poison, neglect of twin-mothers, and cruelty to women. Depending on the offense, some received months of hard labor or a stern lecture warning of severe punishment for future offenses. For some, she imposed fines. Those who could not pay, Mary took to her home, gave them work, a meal, and talked with them about God.

At night, she wrote court reports to the British consul. Natives walked from as far away as a hundred miles, as Mary's reputation for fairness spread.

Court began with the witnesses taking the mbiam pot oath. Surrounded by skulls, the chief dipped a stick into a pot and spread a mixture of blood and dirt on the witness's feet, arms, head, and tongue. The natives believed the mbiam oath would kill anyone who lied. The stench filled the air as the witness repeated the oath, "If I am guilty of this crime . . ."

One-by-one, the witnesses were introduced to Mary. The local chiefs sat with her as part of the court, but Mary ruled supreme. Mary patiently knitted while each side explained its case. If the chiefs interrupted, they received a warning. If they interrupted again, Mary rose and boxed their ears. Those who challenged her earned a whack with her court slippers.

One day Mary learned about a dispute between two men from different tribes.

"Both men claim the same land. Who is telling the truth?" the chief said.

"Bring the men to me," Mary said, holding up her Bible. "You shake with fear, but you need not fear. I judge with God's Word—Iko Abasi."

Several hours later, after patiently listening to each man explain his side, Mary resolved the first dispute. Because she understood the natives' customs and the subtle meanings of their expressions, their lies did not fool her. "Who sacrifices on the land?" Mary waited for the tribal chief to answer. "That is the tribe that owns the land."

The chief thrust another man in front of her. "Imprison him." He pushed the man forward. "He owes many brass rods and cannot pay."

Mary thought about the debtors' prisons in Scotland. She remembered her mother who'd given up everything to keep the family out of debt and how she'd worked in the mill to help.

Mary softly spoke to the accused man. "What do you own?"

He shrugged. "Nothing but a cow."

"Bring your cow to me."

Mary laid the brass rods she owned in the man's hand. "I own the cow now. Go and pay your debt."

Ma's coo is what the natives called the cow, especially when it ran away from its yard. The runaway cow, an occasional leopard, or Mary on her bicycle were the only ones who used the new road. Realizing how much faster she could travel, Mary rode her bicycle often.

She built another mission in Use, recommended that the mission board build a hospital in Itu, and moved to Use. Mary loved the new spot and built several little mud-huts, hoping she could begin a training center for girls someday.

She looked out over the gorgeous hilltop lined with cotton trees and palms and wondered why God had trusted her with so much. *I am so honored, Lord.*

One rainy day, Chief Onoyom visited Mary in Use. "Ma, our entire town is under water. The new church flooded. The people say I brought a curse on our land by building with the juju tree."

Mary couldn't tell if the water dripping down Onoyom's face was rain or tears. "Onoyom, God is pushing you toward greater things. Find higher ground and build a tidy, new town."

Encouraged, Onoyom left the next day determined to rebuild with the juju wood and ignore the superstitious talk.

Onoyom wasn't the only one to visit. Not long after Onoyom's visit, a stranger appeared in Mary's yard. Dressed in native fashion, the man didn't look like any tribe she had ever seen.

She was further away from help than she had ever been. Who was this man?

The young man dressed in a loin cloth led several more men into Mary's yard. "Mökömö Ma, I salute you. I am Udü and have come from the town Ikpe."

Mary had never heard of Ikpe. "Where is that?"

"Two days up the creek. A village with a large market."

Mary kept questioning the visitor. "I've never seen the trading canoes go that direction."

"No, we don't trade with Calabar."

"Ah, a closed market."

"We want to learn book from you."

Janie joined the conversation. "Ma can't travel so far."

Mary knew she was getting feeble and nodded. "I have the mission here to look after."

"We want to be God-men. We will build a church."

Mary couldn't forge through creeks and hike for miles to far-off villages anymore. "Stay and I will teach you. Then you can teach your village."

The group of young men stayed for days listening to the Bible stories before they returned to Ikpe.

The next few nights were restless for Mary. "I can't stop thinking about the Ikpe men," Mary said to Janie as they sat around the fire.

Janie put her hands on her hips. "*Ma.*"

Mary winked at Janie. "I have to go."

"They're too primitive. You're too old to walk for miles."

"God will take care of this old body. They want to learn book, Janie." Mary waved her compass in the air. "Janie, it's an adventure in Christ."

"Ma, you'll be going back to twin-killings and the old customs again."

25

Ikpe

1908

Two days later, after miles on Enyong Creek and another day's trek through the forest, Mary, with the help of another missionary, Martha Peacock, found Ikpe.

They entered the village by the market. A tree carved with distorted faces stood at the entrance. Blood-soaked feathers, a dead monkey's paw, and chicken bones tied with snake skin littered the ground by the carving.

The market was filled with a variety of vegetables and fruits and even animal skulls for trading. Women wearing nothing but bangles and beads stopped their work as Mary passed.

Instead of running and hiding, naked children followed Mary while she searched for the man, Udü.

In the center of the village, a clay figure sat atop a mud altar. Three white headless chickens hung above the altar. Scores of human skulls lined the ground.

Mosquitoes and flies swarmed in and out of the dark huts. "Martha, this is the most heathen place I've ever seen."

They found Udü working on a mud hut. "Ma Slessor! We knew you would come. We have already started the church with a room for you."

"What is the wooden carving on the tree at the entrance?"

"Ndem. Our people sacrifice and eat animals to the idol Ndem. They believe he will make their yams grow big."

"I am so glad I came. Only God grants such blessings."

Mary spent several days discovering villages tucked away close to Ikpe. She worked with Udü on the church, carrying sand, mudding, and rubbing the new walls.

Mary was convinced she had to help the people of Ikpe. "There's so much work to be done, Martha. We'll travel back and forth until the mission board sends more help."

After a few days of teaching in Ikpe, Mary returned to Use to her bed to recover. As soon as she gained strength, Mary wrote letters to Duke Town begging for help.

"We need missionaries to help build a mission in Ikpe, so I can continue serving in Use. Both areas are crying out for help. When I leave one, the other village is without a shepherd. The people deserve to hear the story of salvation. I counted eight-hundred women on the beach welcoming the men who'd been hunting. There are thousands and thousands of people here."

Over and over she made the trip. Each trip, she discovered more villages.

Finally, Mary decided to move to Ikpe. She hauled corrugated iron sheets, wood, nails, and trunks of cement powder on the canoe for the mission.

As soon as she arrived, Udü informed Mary that two women had been beheaded on the way to the market. And the chief had fined and flogged the new Christian boys for not joining the village's drama, called ekang. Other Christians were punished for refusing to eat the animal sacrifices to the idol Ndem.

Mary shook her head. "I dreamed last night that we won this entire region for Jesus. I must go up against the chiefs and stop these barbaric customs." Mary looked to the sky. *Help me win them for You, Jesus.*

The elderly chiefs, their skin withered and looking dehydrated like the cinnamon-brown pods on the trees, listened to Mary, but ignored her pleas. Over months, after many prayers and much patience, Mary won the chiefs' hearts, and they agreed to learn God's ways.

A few years earlier, the mission board had built a hospital in Itu and named it the Mary Slessor Hospital. The mission board did not have a missionary to send to help Mary in Ikpe, but in 1911 they sent the new missionary doctor at Itu, Dr. John Hitchcock, to check on Mary.

After a few days, Dr. Hitchcock shared his conclusions with Mary. "Miss Slessor, I've learned two things. One, you are charming. And two . . . you are too old for this work. A sixty-three-year-old body should not continue to do what you're doing. The mission board is concerned about your health, Miss Slessor. I insist you return to Use."

Mary sat on the dirt floor, leaning against the hut for support. "If I didn't like you so much, Dr. Hitchcock, I'd tell you that you're too young to be bossing . . ." Mary sighed and looked at her wrinkled hands. "I will respect your opinion, Dr. Hitchcock. I am getting feeble."

Mary left thirty-five-year-old Janie in charge of the church in Ikpe. Janie had promised to work like her mother, mixing cement and hauling water and teaching the Bible. Mary checked on Udü before she left. "Remain faithful, Udü. God will perform miracles."

The paddlers carried Mary through the sloshy mud and through the thick jungle and to the waiting canoe.

In Use, the storms had damaged the mission. Trees had fallen, doors had been torn from their hinges, and roof sections had been ripped away. Feverish and weak, Mary spent days in bed recovering from the trip.

As soon as Mary could stand, she patched the holes in her roof with putty before the next storm arrived. After hours of work in the scorching sun, her hands were cracked and bleeding.

Mary stopped to rest for a moment, turned and saw a man approaching. She saw that his helmet was a British officer's sun helmet. "Let me help you," the officer said.

"Just another minute, laddie. A tornado damaged the roof, and I'm almost finished patching." Mary wiped her forehead. "The sun's fierce today. I . . ."

"Miss Slessor. Miss Slessor!"

Mary collapsed.

The officer transported Mary to the Mary Slessor Hospital in Itu, but it was difficult to convince her to stay.

"A day's rest is enough. I'm ready to leave, Dr. Hitchcock."

"What's your hurry, Miss Slessor? If you don't rest, you'll collapse again. If the officer hadn't been there, you would have fallen to your death. I intend to keep you here until your fever goes away. Now, take a peek out your window. There's a gift out there for you."

"A cart?"

"Yes, a cart. No more bicycle for you, my friend. You're crippled with arthritis, Miss Slessor."

"I get along fine, Dr. Hitchcock."

"And you need some food in that bony body of yours. Miss Slessor, you must promise to eat more."

"I eat the native herbs, some fish, and vegetables from the market." She shrugged.

"How about a vacation?"

She shook her head no. "There's too much to do."

"If you don't stop working so hard, your body is going to quit. Ikpe is an unsuitable place for you to live. It's a swamp full of mosquitoes."

"But . . ."

"Miss Slessor." Dr. Hitchcock thumped his stethoscope against his chest. "As your doctor," his voice softened, "as a man who loves you like a son, you can't go back to Ikpe. This is a life-or-death decision."

26

A Rest

1912

After her hospital stay, Mary felt better and visited Janie in Ikpe, but she was back in Use by the time Dr. Hitchcock came to check on her.

"Dr. Hitchcock, how wonderful to see you." Mary sat on her veranda rocking a baby.

"Miss Slessor, you went to Ikpe against my recommendation."

"I had to see my Ikpe family. The chiefs flog the Christians when I'm not there. The boys carried me in my basket chair."

"Did you eat the cooked chicken I sent?"

"I'm not a meat-eater." She paused and smiled. "Yes, we enjoyed it for supper."

Hitchcock smiled. "I want you eating meat twice a day. Now, no more traveling, or I'm going to take you back to the hospital with me."

"I said my goodbyes in Ikpe. I am feeling feeble, but it makes me want to push harder instead of rest. My time is running out."

"And you've opened another mission house in Odoro Ikpe?"

"They're all so receptive to God's Word. I can't ignore them when they ask."

The afternoon melted away while Mary and Dr. Hitchcock talked.

"Even though I've defied you many times," Mary said, "You are a true Christian, a doctor who ministers to both the physical and the spiritual."

Every other day, Dr. Hitchcock walked to Use to check on Mary.

"Miss Slessor, it is time for your next furlough."

"Who will do the work? I can't leave."

"You'll be more productive after a rest. You have a friend who would like to provide a vacation for you to the Grand Canary Islands. Take Janie with you."

"It feels selfish."

"It's necessary, not selfish. How many years have you been a missionary?"

"Let's see, laddie. I came to Duke Town in 1876." Mary stopped to think. "Why that's thirty-six years. I can hardly believe it."

"And you have a yard full of children. How many children have you raised in thirty-six years?" Dr. Hitchcock asked.

Mary watched the children playing. "I've adopted two more, Whitie and Asuquo. That makes nine children I've adopted. I'm very proud of my children. They're all Christians. Annie teaches in Nkana, a village near Ikpe, with her husband. Janie is taking over most of my work. And Alice and Maggie are old enough to help Janie now.

"Children come and go," Mary continued. "Many of the children I've cared for have been adopted by other Christians. Some children started teaching in different villages when they were old enough." She paused and smiled. "In Akpap, I had nine babies at one time. Over the years, I'd say fifty different children have been rescued. Sometimes I felt like the old woman in the shoe who had so many children she didn't know what to do." Mary laughed.

Dr. Hitchcock smiled. "You are old, Miss Slessor. Give your body a vacation. You have friends and grown daughters who will help."

"Only if you promise I can do double the work when I return."

"Mary, the rest is a must. Your heart muscle is weak."

Sixty-four-year-old Mary spent a glorious month in the Canary Islands at the Hotel Santa Catalina and then returned to Use. Despite her wrinkled skin and the hobble in her walk, she planned life with as much enthusiasm as she had as a young missionary. The restful trip had improved her health, and she launched into her dreams of building schools and churches in all of Ibibio territory.

Mary compared the changes from when she'd first worked as a missionary to now. Dirt roads replaced worn paths. British officers carried more authority than village chiefs. The British government promised Mary every convenience a British officer would have at his disposal, including a government motorcar. The car created possibilities for spreading God's Word faster and farther.

Feeble in body but determined to minister to her church family in Ikpe, Mary traveled by motorcar on the new government road from Ikot Ekpene to reach Ikpe faster. When they reached the road's end, Mary had to get into her cart to continue to Ikpe. The government car drove away, spraying mud from its tires. Mud splattered Mary's face and pelleted her eye. She wiped herself clean and continued on to Ikpe.

The village didn't look the same as when she had started teaching in Ikpe three years earlier. People walked past clothed and tidy. No decaying food, dead animal's bones, or feces cluttered the paths. A group of women gathered near a spring to wash clothes. Clothes hung over tree branches to dry in the hot sun. All around, children splashed and played in the spring.

The next day was Sunday, and Mary conducted church services as tears flowed involuntarily from her injured eye. Her face was covered with orange-colored swollen patches. Concerned, the village clamored to help Mary.

"It's just a small accident. Don't make a fuss over me. It will clear up."

But native workers reported Mary's injury to the British officers outside of Ikpe. Immediately, a mounted officer took off to Ikpe. "Bring Miss Slessor to the nearest point of the road for a car."

Even though it was market day the next morning, the church members in the village helped Mary meet the government car. By now, her eyelid was swollen shut, and she couldn't see anything from her injured eye.

The local district commissioner and a doctor waited for Mary at the meeting point with medicine and then returned her to Use.

When Mary reached Use, Dr. Hitchcock visited and took her to the hospital and consulted another physician, Dr. Parkinson.

The sun streamed through the window, but Mary couldn't see anything with her left eye. Only darkness. Tears streamed from her throbbing eye. Mary didn't want to admit it, but she'd never felt so miserable.

"This is more serious than you realize. You've developed a serious infection called erysipelas. How's the pain, Miss Slessor?" Dr. Parkinson asked, as Dr. Hitchcock stood nearby.

"If I let discomfort stop me, I would never get anything done. Pain is my constant companion." Mary shrugged. She lived with arthritis and a weak heart. Boils, vomiting, and fevers stopped her temporarily, but she'd always recovered. Now, her body felt like a flickering candle, but she wouldn't stop working. There was so much work to be done. So many people to reach for Jesus.

Dr. Parkinson administered more medicine, with Dr. Hitchcock assisting him. Dr. Parkinson cleared his throat. "I'm sorry. I can't promise you'll be able to see from your left eye again. It's important for you to rest both eyes, Miss Slessor."

Dr. Hitchcock smiled. "I've explained to Dr. Parkinson how difficult it is to make you rest. But you must, if you want your eye to heal." Dr. Hitchcock shook his finger. "Here's your prescription. Don't go to that mosquito infested swamp again."

All her life, she'd been sloshing in mud and muck and now, had it ruined her sight? Was thirty-seven years of mission work over?

Mary spent her days writing letters to friends and confessed the eye accident had put her near "the valley of the shadow of death." She prayed every time her worries returned. *God are You ending my work?* She prayed for His healing, His will.

27

In Akpap Again

1913

Two weeks later, Mary's fever left, the infection cleared, and her vision returned, but the eye trouble continued.

"Doctor, it feels like the swollen area is moving. Can it be worms?"

"The nerves in your eye haven't recovered," Dr. Parkinson said.

Two months passed before Mary's eye returned to normal. During her recovery she received an invitation to the opening of a new church in Akpap. She realized how much she missed her sister Eme Ete, and she arranged for her son-in-law, David, to drive her to Akpap. He was a government driver. Mary's sons, Dan and Asuquo, were in Calabar attending the Hope Waddell Training Institute for boys, so Mary's grown daughters traveled to Akpap with her.

The landscaped blurred as the government car sped past the countryside Mary had tramped through so many times. She looked down at her gnarled hands and swollen feet, thankful for modern conveniences like automobiles and medicine. As much as she didn't want to admit it, her body felt fatigued.

A crowd formed around the car as David opened the door for Mary.

"Ma. Eka Kpukpru Owo!" people shouted as they recognized their Ma. Immediately women clamored around to compliment her, rubbing her arms and hair. Mary remembered her early days as a missionary and how this act of affection scared her. *My, how much I've changed,* she thought.

The crowd grew larger as Mary hugged old friends. After a few minutes, she nudged David's arm.

David escorted her over the rusty-colored trail into the village, past thatched huts and stick fences, searching for Ma Eme. A group of giggling children abandoned their playful pursuit of a goat to follow Mary.

Mary found Eme sitting in the shade outside her hut, waving away flies. A huge turban covered Eme's head. Mary recognized the twisted cloth—a brilliant blue material she'd brought from Scotland and given to Eme years earlier. Charms of claws, feathers, and shells hung around her hut. On top of an altar, palm wine and food offerings lay next to a mud idol. Mary's heart soared at seeing her friend but sank knowing Ma Eme still worshiped an idol.

For such a large woman, Eme seemed to catapult from the chair, her face gleaming, eyes glistening. "Mary Slessor, you are finally here!" Eme's stubby hands patted Mary's. "I didn't believe I would see your face again." Ma Eme turned to the curious young women nearby, clicked her tongue and snapped her fingers. "Get the cooking pots and the fires ready. We will celebrate. Our dear Ma is here."

The drummers announced Mary's arrival. Children danced around the fire while Ma Eme and Mary shared a calabash of water and nibbled on seeds and nuts. They talked for hours under the shade of a palm tree.

"Old women we are, Eme."

Ma Eme fingered the beads around her neck. "We are."

"We've shared many secrets, many miracles."

"We have."

"I won't likely see you again, Eme." Knowing Eme had never become a Christian, Mary felt desperate. She had to ask her once more. "Eme, will I see you in heaven with the Great Chief?"

Ma Eme fingered the bead necklace that hung around her neck, sat stiff, and didn't answer.

Mary's plea turned to a whisper. "You're my sister, Eme. I pray for you every day."

Ma Eme stood. "Come. The soup is prepared."

Oh dear Lord, will You open my sister's heart and allow her to accept Your love and sacrifice of Your Son?

During the next few days, Mary visited with the new missionaries at Akpap, played with the children, and helped the sick. On Sunday, she preached in the four-hundred-member church. The last day of her visit, she rose as the blue haze curled in the air from the early morning cooking fires.

When Mary reached Eme's hut, she gasped. A white silk cloth covered Ma Eme's door—the sign of death. Mary fell to her knees crying. "Eme . . . Eme."

David clutched Mary's hand and led her to the car. She shared her grief with Janie on the way home. "Oh, how I will miss Ma Eme. She still practiced the heathen idol worship. We have to work harder and pray harder." Mary sniffed and wiped her eyes.

"We lived in Ekenge and Akpap with Eme Ete for fifteen years. Yet, my dear sister never accepted Christ. I wanted to see her again . . . in heaven. Mark your Bible when you read, memorize the Scriptures. God's Word is our living water, our bread of life. Without it we have no hope of eternal life. Write what God is teaching you in the margins."

Mary looked out at the miles and miles of unexplored jungle. "Look at this country. There's so much to do. "

Back home in Use, Mary continued her work, but she moved at a slower pace. Although her body was beaten down by the years of work and heartbroken over the loss of her sister, Mary remained firm in her commitment to carry God's good news to lost people.

One day a messenger delivered Mary a box from Scotland. She rummaged through the box, looking for the usual letters and newspapers. She'd been without any news for seven weeks.

The newspapers confirmed the rumors she'd heard. Britain and France were at war with Germany. *That's why the trading on the river has slowed down*, she thought. She felt like her heart would drop—war in Europe. She had hoped war would not happen.

Curious, Mary tore open an important-looking envelope. She had been invited to Duke Town by the British government to receive a silver cross. But Mary forgot about the invitation until a few days later when another messenger arrived.

"There is going to be a program to honor your work, Miss Slessor. I have orders to bring you to Duke Town."

"I'd prefer for this to remain a private matter."

"Miss Slessor, this is a royal medal from England."

"God is the one who needs to be honored. I pray that accepting the medal will make more people aware of the mission work."

Mary packed the frock she wore to the Canary Islands, but it was moldy from rain. At the Duke Town mission house, she rummaged through a trunk of hand-me-down clothes from Scotland until she finally collected a purple sweater, a yellow skirt, and a straw hat.

Mary paused as she looked in a mirror, seeing a worn-out piece of parchment, no milk-and-roses complexion anymore. She remembered the years when she could cut a trail through the jungle as fast as any African. Her feet were too wide for shoes now, so she slipped on her old court slippers.

That evening, an officer led Mary to Goldie Hall. She felt her legs shake. She felt out of place among the officers, missionaries, and dignitaries.

The provincial commissioner, Mr. Bedwell, began the ceremony. "This remarkable lady thought she was working in Africa unnoticed, but her story had to be shared. Mary Slessor has saved hundreds of twins, pioneered in territory no white man would dare enter, and negotiated peace in former slave-trading tribes." He cleared his throat and looked at Mary.

She nervously clutched her skirt in her hands and looked at her feet. She didn't want any attention. All she ever wanted was to be the feet of the church and to wear the shoes of peace into Africa.

Mr. Bedwell escorted Mary to the front and then continued his speech. "News of her work has won the attention of King George V. This honor is bestowed on those who work to relieve the sick and suffering. By the Order of the Hospital of St. John of Jerusalem, I honor you with the Silver Cross." His golden epaulettes, sword hilt, and red sash shone against his white uniform.

Mary looked at the audience. *Oh, how I'd rather be standing in front of my dear black brothers and sisters singing hymns under the silvery moonlight*, she thought.

"Miss Slessor." He offered Mary the podium.

Mary breathed deeply and held onto his arm. *I haven't done anything. God, You've done it all. Help me say something wise, God.*

"'Tis an honor, but I accept this on behalf of the mission which has been my privilege to serve. Anything I have done in my life has been easy," Mary paused, "because the Master has gone before me. Thank you."

While the audience rose and applauded, Mary stepped away from the podium, her arm tucked around Commissioner Bedwell's and a bouquet of roses. Amid the applause, she looked at the uniformed officers and wondered what would become of the dear laddies with a war raging in Europe?

Mary left Duke Town with a silver cross and an aching heart. Once more there would be war instead of peace, bloodshed instead of forgiveness. The work—His work and hers—would never end. *I must pray more. I must continue preaching the gospel.*

Epilogue

1913–1915

As soon as Mary arrived home, she planted a rose stem from the bouquet. Two years after Mary received the Silver Cross, the rose bush had flourished, but Mary contracted a fever and had to be carried from Ikpe to Use. In the hut at Use, ants had eaten through a milk box, rats had eaten clothes, and dirt covered everything. Too sick to work, Mary sent word for Miss Peacock to come help Janie. Martha Peacock arrived in September with a camp bed for Mary to sleep on, instead of the cement floor.

When the mail came by canoe or car, Mary read the discouraging news of the British and French defeats. She often spent days in bed with pain and fever over the next year. When she felt well enough, she'd travel back and forth from Use to help in Odoro Ikpe, Endot, and Ekir Mornu.

On December 24, 1914, she wrote a letter to Charles Partridge.

> *My Dear Old Friend,*
> *The plum pudding arrived. It's taking all my self-control not to spoon a bit right this minute, but the family will enjoy it tonight for Christmas Eve. If I can hold on, I plan a rest in Scotland or the Canaries in March . . .*

In January, Mary collapsed and slipped in and out of consciousness for days. Miss Peacock sent for a doctor. Throughout the day and night of January 12, Janie, Annie,

Alice, Maggie, and Whitie took turns watching Mary. Her bony body shrank as her life ebbed away. She tossed and twisted on the cot, trying to find relief. Janie wiped Mary's forehead and lips with a wet cloth. Sweating, babbling, and struggling to breathe, Mary whispered, "Thanks, lassie, but it's nae use." In the early hours of January 13, Mary prayed, "O Abasi, sana mi yok. God release me from my pain."

The cries of Mary's children echoed through the village. Messengers ran to spread the sad news. In response to their grief, natives wailed, beat their chests, and tore their clothes. Then *boom, boom, boom . . .* the news spread through the forest. *Eka Kpukpru Owo,* the mother of us all, has died.

During the night, the steamer *Snipe* floated Mary's body from the Cross River into the Calabar River for the last time. Before sunrise, Efik, Okoyong, Itu, Enyong, Aro, and Ibibio natives arrived in their torch-lit canoes to honor their Ma. A band played the national anthem; soldiers drew their swords and formed an arch as Mary's mahogany coffin was lifted from the boat.

On January 15, 1915, flags waved at half-mast, and schools and offices were closed while local missionaries, government officials, native tribes, and students from the Hope Waddell Institute and the Duke Town School gathered for the funeral. From the dock to the mission house, police saluted as British officers carried her coffin.

As the bright sun cleared the pearly dawn sky, the procession walked a mile and a half from the beach to the cemetery. First, the high commissioner, then the missionaries, and finally other British and government officials. At the cemetery, former head-hunters, slave traders, and cannibals wept quietly. Children climbed trees to peek above the crowd.

On a hilltop cemetery near the Duke Town mission house, Mary's coffin was buried over a former slave pit, next to the Andersons. The Union Jack and a cross of pink frangipani blossoms covered the coffin.

The tough and tender mill girl turned missionary, pioneer, preacher, and warrior for God finally rested.

God had fulfilled her dream. Mary Slessor served God for thirty-nine years, spreading Christianity through the jungles of Africa.

Terms

biscuit: a Scottish cookie made of flour, butter, and sugar

consul: a representative of a government.

cut oath: men cut hands and rub blood to together to symbolically show agreement

Da': Scottish word for Dad

eseré: a poison bean

elder: a high-ranking representative of a tribe

frangipani: fragrant flower

furlough: vacation or break from duty

gig: small canoe

harmatten: blowing sands from November through February from the Sahara desert

long ju-ju: a shrine to the Aro god, Chukwu

mort cloth: a black cloth used to cover a coffin

palaver: meeting or meeting hut

parchment: stiff old paper made from animal skins

petticoat: a woman's undergarment, like a slip

plum pudding: a rich boiled pudding of raisins, dried fruits, and spices

poultice: a moist cloth filled with herbs to apply to wounds for medicinal purposes

shortbread: a Scottish butter cookie